STEALING HOME

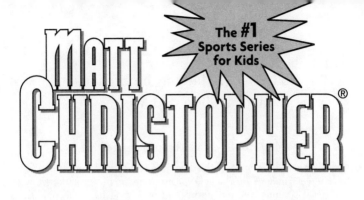

MATT CHRISTOPHER®

STEALING HOME

Text by Paul Mantell

LITTLE, BROWN AND COMPANY

New York · An AOL Time Warner Company

To Clay and Matt, my inspiration,
and, as always, to Avery.

Text by Paul Mantell

First Edition

The characters and events in this book are fictitious. Any similarity to real
persons, living or dead, is coincidental and not intended by the author.

Library of Congress Cataloging-in-Publication Data

Mantell, Paul.
    Stealing home / text by Paul Mantell. — 1st ed.
        p. cm.
    Summary: Joey is sure he will not get along with the exchange student
from Nicaragua who is staying with his family for a year, but they find
common ground on the baseball field.
    ISBN 0-316-60739-8 (hc) / ISBN 0-316-60742-8 (pb)
    [1. Student exchange programs — Fiction.   2. Baseball — Fiction.
3. Nicaraguans — Fiction.   4. Schools — Fiction.   5. Friendship —
Fiction.   6. Family life — Fiction.]   I. Title.

PZ7.M31835St 2004
[Fic] — dc22   2003047712

            HC: 10 9 8 7 6 5 4 3 2 1
            PB: 10 9 8 7 6 5 4 3 2 1

                    Q-FF (hc)
                    COM-MO (pb)

Printed in the United States of America

STEALING HOME

1

Joey Gallagher bounced up and down on the balls of his feet. He pounded his mitt with his right fist and stared in toward home plate from deep center field, ready to catch the ball that came his way.

Nicky Canelo, the Marlins pitcher, reared back and fired the ball so hard that he went airborne for a second. The Oriole batter, with his bright-orange helmet, swung a second too late. The ball smacked into the catcher's mitt, sending up a cloud of powdery dust. The batter fell to his knees in a twisted, frustrated heap.

"Stee-rike two!" the umpire yelled. Parents clapped and yelled on both sides of the field. Joey bounced up and down on the balls of his feet some more and looked around him. In left field, Huey Brewster had his glove hand on his hip. Ellis Suggs, in right, was digging a hole in the outfield grass with his cleats. "What is he doing, looking for worms?" Joey asked himself disgustedly.

Neither of the other two outfielders looked prepared. And why should they be? None of the Orioles was going to hit Nicky Canelo's fastball. Nobody ever did. Still, it was important to be ready. Joey shook his head and turned his attention back toward the plate. Nicky went into his windup and fired another unhittable blur.

"Stee-rike three! Yer out!" the umpire said with gusto. It was impossible not to appreciate Nicky's awesome talent, even if umpires weren't supposed to take sides. The batter threw down his bat in disgust and marched back to the bench.

Nicky Canelo stepped off the mound, all six-foot-one of him. He whirled his pitching arm round and round like a windmill, keeping it loose. Too bad league rules didn't let teams use one pitcher all the time. The Marlins could use Nicky only for three innings per six-inning game.

The first three innings . . . well, those were the Marlins' biggest problem. Starter Matt Lowe was pretty accurate, but he got hit around a lot. The Marlins could only hope to stay close till Nicky took the mound in the fourth inning. If they were ahead by then, it was curtains for the other team.

Like today. They were up, 2–0, with two outs in the bottom of the fourth inning. One more batter — then two more innings — and the Marlins would be 4–0. A perfect record. Sure, the season was young, and a lot could still happen, but so far Coach Joe Bacino had come up with the perfect formula for success. "Hang on for three, then bring on Nick-eee!"

Three wins, no losses. And the last three innings of each game, with Nicky on the mound, had been mad boring for all the Marlins fielders. Nobody got any action except Pete Alessandra, the catcher.

Joey had lots of time to think out there in center field. He thought about last year, in sixth grade, when he'd pitched and played shortstop for the Mets. This year, he'd moved up a league. Most of the Marlins were eighth graders, much bigger than he was. Joey felt lucky — at least he got to play most of every game. The other seventh graders usually rode the bench till "Nicky time" and never saw any balls hit to them at all. Still, Joey kept bouncing. "Gotta stay ready. Never know when you're gonna get your big chance," he muttered under his breath.

The next hitter came up for the Orioles. It was their "big bat," Andy Norton. Joey was friends with him, sort of — they were both seventh graders, and they had history, English, and gym together. Joey knew that Andy was leading the league in home runs because Andy never missed the chance to brag about it. Joey couldn't wait to see Nicky Canelo strike him out.

"Keep on bouncin', keep on bouncin'," he sang softly to himself. "Gotta stay ready. Never know when it's comin' to you."

Yeah, right. Like anyone was ever gonna hit Nicky . . .

And then, in an instant, everything changed. Andy Norton squeezed his eyes shut and swung. *SMACK!* The bat hit the ball dead on. It rocketed toward the mound, where it hit Nicky right in the pitching arm. There was a sickening sound on impact, and the ball ricocheted all the way to first base.

Charlie Morganstern picked it up and stepped on the bag to end the inning, but no one was watching — not even the umpire. Everyone was crowding around the mound, where Nicky Canelo had fallen in a heap. Joey could hear Coach Bacino yelling for someone to call 911 and asking if there was a doctor in the stands.

Joey was so surprised that someone had hit the ball that it was a full ten seconds before he raced toward the mound. He got there just in time to see Nicky being helped to his feet. The Marlins' star pitcher was sobbing, grabbing his arm with his glove hand.

Joey was stunned. It must be bad, if a kid like Nicky Canelo was crying. They walked him over to the bench and put a cold pad on the spot where the ball had hit. Nicky was calmer now, but you could still see him sniffing back tears. Sirens sounded in the distance. Joey edged closer. Now he could see the ugly, swollen, purple bruise on Nicky's upper arm.

"He can make a fist and bend the elbow," said one of the parents. "That's a good sign, but he'll still have to get x-rayed to make sure nothing's broken."

Nicky's teammates clapped for him as Coach Bacino led him to the ambulance. Everyone wished him good luck at the hospital. "I'll be okay," he assured them bravely. "Hey, you guys — win this one for me, okay?" They all promised to do just that.

But how? They were only up by two runs, and Matt Lowe had already pitched his three innings.

"Okay, who's gonna pitch the next two innings?" Coach Bacino asked his team as they gathered around the bench. A sea of willing but incapable hands went up. Joey stuck his hand up, too.

Coach Bacino stroked the little beard on his chin and squinted, looking doubtfully down the line of them. His eyes came to rest on Joey. "Gallagher," he said. "Didn't you say you used to pitch last year?"

"Uh-huh," Joey said.

"Okay, you're it." Coach Bacino put the ball in Joey's mitt and squeezed it with both his hands. "Just get it over the plate. It's okay if they hit it. That's what your fielders are for." Joey nodded and swallowed hard. He rubbed up the ball and tried to remember how he used to pitch way back in the old days, last year. Then he started warming up his arm, soft-tossing the ball to Pete on the sidelines.

The Marlins went down quickly at bat. Before he knew it, it was time to get out on the mound. Funny, but the minute he got up there, he didn't feel nervous anymore. His team had a two-run lead, didn't they? Besides, he felt like he couldn't lose, no matter what happened. If he pitched badly and they lost, he had the perfect excuse: "Hey, I wasn't prepared," he could say. "I didn't have any practice." On the other hand, if he had the least bit of success up there . . .

He focused in on Pete Alessandra's great-big catcher's mitt, reared back, and threw. The hitter swung hard, popped it up, and Charlie Morganstern caught the ball in foul territory. One out already — on only one pitch! Joey drank in his teammates' cheers. They were behind him all the way. He could feel it. He bore down on the next hitter and threw another meatball, right over home plate.

THWACK! A line drive to right field. If it had been Nicky pitching, Ellis Suggs would've been caught napping, digging holes with his cleats in the outfield grass. But because Joey Nobody was on the mound, everyone was ready for anything. Suggs got his carcass moving just in time to make a diving play on the liner, and there were two out.

"All right!" Joey yelled, totally pumped now. If Ellis Suggs could make a play like that, then surely he, Joey Gallagher, could get four more batters out. He threw a change-up on the first pitch to the next hitter and caught the overanxious Oriole off guard. Swinging too soon, he popped up to Joey, and the inning was over.

Joey could scarcely believe it. Three outs on three pitches — and this was in the seventh-/eighth-grade league! Quickly he contained his urge to celebrate.

There was still one more inning to go. He walked to the bench, barely acknowledging his teammates' cheers and backslaps.

The Marlins again went down quickly at the plate. The Orioles weren't 3–0 for nothing. Even if they lost today, they'd still be in second place to the Marlins. Their number-one pitcher was still out there, and while he was no Nicky Canelo, he was still pretty tough to hit.

Joey got back on the mound and blew out a big, deep breath. This was it. This could be his day of glory — to remember forever. All he had to do was get three outs before the Orioles scored two runs.

The first batter fouled off six pitches and finally worked out a walk. The next batter lined a sharp single up the middle. The runner on first put on the gas. Before Joey knew what had hit him, there were Orioles on first and third, with the top of the order coming up, and he still needed three outs!

Coach Bacino trotted out to talk to him. "You okay, kid?" he asked.

"I'm okay."

"Are you gonna get this next guy out?"

"Uh-huh."

"How you gonna do that?"

"I'm uh . . . I'm gonna make him hit it," Joey said, remembering.

"That's right. You can't get three outs at once. Just get 'em one at a time. And never mind that run on third base. It means nothing. Just throw it over the plate. We don't want Alessandra digging pitches out of the dirt. Next thing you know, the guy on first is stealing second and getting in scoring position. So throw some strikes. Okay?"

"Okay."

"Go get 'em."

Joey blew out another big breath. He stared at Pete's catcher's mitt and threw a really slow change-up. The hitter's eyes nearly popped out of his head as he swung, but he was way too early. The ball was only halfway to the plate. He'd finished his swing completely before it even hit the catcher's mitt.

"Stee-rike one!" the umpire yelled.

"Try that again, you wimp!" the batter called to him.

"Yeah?" Joey yelled back. "You want another one?" He reared back and threw as hard and high as he dared. The batter, taken totally by surprise, swung at air again.

"Stee-rike two!" the umpire said.

"All right," the batter said, spitting in the dirt. "You're dead meat now." He waggled his bat over his shoulder. Now Joey threw him the second change-up he'd promised him, and this one was even slower than the first.

The batter started his swing, then stopped it midway when he realized what was coming. He tried to restart his swing, but there was so little force left behind it that he hit a soft grounder right back to the mound. Joey grabbed it, turned, and threw to second. Shortstop Jordan Halpin took the throw, stepped on the bag ahead of the runner, then threw to first in plenty of time for the double play.

"Yes!" Joey screamed, throwing his mitt high in the air. The game wasn't over yet, though, and the runner on third had scored to make it a 2–1 game. Still, the bases were empty, and if he got this batter out, or even the next one, he wouldn't have to face Andy Norton. Joey went after the hitter, throwing nothing but fastballs. On the third one, the Oriole hit a harmless grounder to Charlie Morganstern, who stepped on the bag to end the game.

Sweet.

"We won! We won! I can't believe it! We won!" all the Marlins shouted. They mobbed Joey at the mound, picked him up, and marched him around the infield on their shoulders — Joey the Hero. Yes, the short, skinny kid with the freckles, the puny seventh grader who put it to the Orioles when Nicky Canelo went down. It was only one day in his life, but try as he might, Joey could not remember a better one.

Coach Bacino gathered the Marlins around him afterward. "Okay, guys, this was a great victory," he said as he put away the team's equipment. "But we've got a lot of baseball to play yet this season, and we may be without Nicky for a lot of it — maybe all of it. For now, Gallagher's our second pitcher." A big round of applause greeted this news. "If we all keep playing like this, we'll still make the play-offs. Let's do it for Nicky!"

Everyone cheered, exchanged high fives, then ran toward the line of cars that was waiting at the curb. Joey, still practically floating, headed for his mom's old bomb of a station wagon. Wait till he told her what happened!

"Hi, Mom!" he said, hurtling himself into the seat beside her.

"Hi, honey!" she said, giving him a quick hug and kiss. "Guess what?"

"Um, I don't know," he said, thrown off. "Hey, Mom, I just —"

"The papers came through, Joey!"

"The papers?"

"Yes, isn't that exciting? We're picking up your new brother next week!"

2

My new brother?

It took Joey a minute to figure out what she was talking about. It wasn't *really* a new brother — only an exchange student, coming to live with them for the summer and the next school year.

"Would you stop saying that?" he pleaded. "He's not my brother, okay?"

"Sorry," she quickly backtracked. "But seriously, aren't you excited? It's really happening!"

He slumped down in the passenger seat and closed his eyes. As his mom steered the car toward home, Joey flashed back to the night his parents had first brought up the matter.

"You know, I'll bet you're missing Sandy a lot, aren't you, Joey?" his dad asked. Sandy, Joey's older brother, had left for college a month earlier.

"Of course he is," his mom said quickly, answering for Joey like she always did. "How could he not miss his big brother?"

"Here's something interesting," his dad said, pointing to an ad in the magazine he was reading. "Host families wanted for exchange students, ten to sixteen years old." He looked up, staring straight at Joey. "We could have a boy your age from another country come and stay with us for a whole year. What do you think about that?"

"Wow, what a great opportunity!" his mom interjected before Joey could even open his mouth. "We could learn each other's languages, and Joey'd have a brother his own age."

"Yes, Sandy was always so much older," his dad agreed. "It wasn't like they could be best buddies all the time."

But Sandy *had* been his best buddy. Even though he was eight years older, and a lot better in school, and not much of an athlete, Sandy had always been a great friend and the person Joey looked up to the most.

Joey had missed Sandy ever since he'd left. But that didn't mean he wanted a replacement brother from who knew where. So he didn't say anything at all, hoping it would blow over and just go away.

As the months went by, his parents had brought up the subject a few more times. But Joey had always just shrugged his shoulders and said he didn't want to talk about it.

And now, two years later, they were telling him it was about to happen? When had he ever given his explicit permission? Didn't he get a vote?

"Well?" his mom asked, glancing at him out of the corner of her eye. "You're being awfully quiet. Aren't you excited?"

He'd been excited a minute ago, all right — excited about winning the big game for his team. But was he excited about getting a "new brother"?

"Not really, Mom, to be perfectly honest" was what he wanted to say. But he didn't say any of that. Instead, he just sighed and said, "So what's this kid's name?"

"I don't know," his mom replied. "Why don't you open the packet and find out?"

Joey hated that his parents pretended they were doing this for him. It was they, not Joey, who missed Sandy so much that they had to bring in another kid to replace him. It was his mom and dad who were inviting a total stranger to be part of their close little family.

"I'll open it when we get home," Joey said.

They arrived at the house. After removing his cleats, dumping his baseball stuff in the bin in the garage, and washing up, Joey went to the kitchen table and opened the packet while his mom heated their dinner. Roast beef. Joey didn't really like roast beef, but what did his mom care about that? Roast beef was Dad's favorite. If his dad was happy, she was happy. It didn't matter what Joey thought. It *never* mattered.

Joey opened the packet, and a bunch of papers spilled out. There was a letter from the supervisor at the exchange organization. There was a handwritten note in Spanish and a photograph in black and white.

A tall boy with curly brown hair and a big, goofy smile stared back at Joey from the photo. The boy was standing under a palm tree on the side of a dusty dirt road. He was waving at the camera. The boy's knees were knobby, and he seemed bowlegged.

Joey read the letter from the head of the exchange program. "Dear Mr. and Mrs. Gallagher and Joey," it began. *Well, at least they know our names,* Joey thought. With every passing second, it was sinking into his brain that this was really about to happen to him. "We are thrilled to pass along the news that your exchange student will be arriving on June 5 at 5:00 P.M. Please be at the airport to greet Jesus Rodriguez."

"Wait a minute," Joey said. "This kid's name is *Jesus?*"

Mrs. Gallagher looked over his shoulder. "Honey, in Spanish cultures, 'Jesus' is a pretty common first name. It's pronounced 'Hey-SOOS.'"

"Oh. 'Hey-SOOS.' Great, that's much better. Mom, don't you think he ought to change his name while he's here, to something more . . . I don't know . . . more normal?"

"Well, honey, what's normal here in Bordentown is different than what's normal in Nicaragua, where Jesus comes from."

"It's weird to be named Jesus," Joey insisted.

"You know, there aren't many people of Spanish or Latino heritage in Bordentown," his mom pointed out. "This isn't a very diverse community. Even though you study Spanish, you can't really speak it, can you? Just think what talking with Jesus will do for your language skills!"

"Great," Joey said. "I still think he should change his

name. You know, when in Rome, do as the Romans do? Ever hear that one?"

"Now, Joey, I'm sure if Jesus feels awkward here, it won't be because of his name. It's our job as his host family to make him feel at home. Remember, we're the ones who volunteered."

We? Joey thought. *Just when exactly did I buy into this?* But, not wanting to get in a fight with his mom about it, he kept his mouth shut and went back to reading the letter:

Jesus is thirteen and is ready to begin eighth grade in September. He has some English, but you may experience some difficulties in communicating at first. There may also be adjustment problems. If so, please let us know, and we will do our best to help smooth things out. We will be checking in on you weekly to make sure everyone is having a positive experience. Thank you again for your willingness to share your lives with a young person from abroad. . . .

Joey picked up the second letter. This one was from Jesus himself. Joey could barely make sense of the handwriting. Then he saw the translation on the second page and breathed a sigh of relief.

"Dear Gallagher family," it began.

Please accept most warm greetings from me and my family. I have three older brothers and two younger sisters, and I am so lucky to be the first one to travel outside Nicaragua. Here the people are mostly poor, but it is very pretty, with good weather and nice people, and it is warm all the time. Do you have snow there? I have never seen snow except in photos and the cinema. I like the cinema, science, and sports. I am so happy I will soon come to stay with you!

Warm greetings, Jesus Rodriguez

Joey put the letter down and stared at the photo again. *Hmmm . . .* Jesus seemed like a normal-enough kid. Of course, you could never tell from a photo. And it wouldn't be like having a brother, no matter what happened. He would only have one brother, ever, and that was Sandy.

His mom placed the salad bowl in the center of the

table. "We're going to have to get the house ready. I thought we'd give Sandy's room to Jesus."

When Sandy had left for college, Joey's parents had asked him whether he wanted to move into Sandy's empty room, which was bigger and had more closets. Joey had refused. It was Sandy's room, not his. But now Joey was sorry that he hadn't made the switch. If Sandy's room was going to be lived in by someone else, at least it should have been him.

Of course, if he said anything now, his mom and dad would accuse him of making a big stink about it and being difficult and immature. "Sandy wouldn't make a big stink," they'd say, and they'd be right. Sandy always did the right thing.

He wished he'd made a big stink when they'd first brought up the idea of an exchange student coming to live with them. Oh well, too late now.

"It'll be great," his mom said, coming over to him and putting an arm around his shoulders. "You'll see. You'll have so much fun showing him everything — school, friends, baseball . . . You're gonna love it."

Joey doubted it. He could picture spending hours and hours tutoring his "new brother" in English in- stead of hanging out and doing cool stuff with his friends. Nobody would want Joey around anymore, because everywhere he went, Jesus would have to come, too. And as for baseball — the kid had probably never even heard of it.

Joey picked up Jesus's letter again. He said he liked sports, but he didn't say which sport. Soccer, maybe? If so, then he and Jesus wouldn't have much to talk about.

Suddenly Joey wondered what they *would* talk about, or if they'd even be able to talk to each other, since Jesus's English didn't seem that good. He pictured the two of them sitting together, totally silent, in Sandy's room. Then, for a split second, he put himself in Jesus's shoes.

It couldn't be easy, being pulled away from your family to go stay with complete strangers in a different country for a whole year. Much as his parents bugged him sometimes, he wasn't sure he'd want to trade them for someone else's.

I guess the least I can do is try to make the guy feel welcome, Joey thought. *And if we don't click, well, no one will be able to blame me.*

3

The next day at school, Joey caught up with his Marlin teammates in the cafeteria at lunch. "Nicky's arm isn't broken," Pete Alessandra told him.

"All right!" Joey said, pumping his fist. "You talked to him?"

"Last night. It's a bad bruise and a confusion or contusion or something like that."

"Man, I thought it was broken for sure," said Charlie Morganstern. "Did you hear that ball hit him? I thought I was gonna puke, it was so sickening."

"Shut up, I'm trying to eat here, you dweeb," Jordan Halpin said, poking Charlie.

"How long's he gonna be out?" Joey asked.

"Three or four weeks," Pete replied. "They told him he's gotta take it easy till the swelling goes down."

"Man, that's like the whole rest of the season," Jordan moaned.

"Don't worry," Joey said. "We're gonna be okay."

"Uh, yeah, listen, I don't wanna jinx you or anything," Charlie said, putting a hand on Joey's shoulder, "but you got those Oriole hitters out with smoke and mirrors."

Joey was stung, even though he knew Charlie meant it as a compliment. "What, you don't think I can do it again?" he asked.

"You'd better!" Pete interjected. "The whole team's counting on it."

"Counting on *you,* Gallagher," Jordan said, ruffling Joey's hair. "You'd better be good. Keep fakin' 'em out."

Joey didn't feel too well all of a sudden. Before yesterday, nobody knew he could pitch, so the Oriole game had been a no-lose situation. Now, it was a no-*win* situation. His teammates were counting on him, even though they thought he'd just gotten lucky last time. They knew — and so did Joey — that he wasn't going to overpower anybody with his fastball. After a while, word would spread around the league, and hitters were going to start figuring him out. Three weeks was a long time to stay one step ahead of them.

On the other hand, if he could somehow manage to do it, Coach Bacino might make him the number-two pitcher behind Nicky, instead of Matt Lowe. Matt threw fast, but he was all over the place. He walked as many batters as he struck out. Joey felt he had a real chance — if he could just hang in there under all the pressure.

"Yeah, you da man now," Pete was saying. "Mr. Junkball to the rescue."

"Mr. Junkball," Larry Levine repeated as he came up to their table, carrying his tray. "Dude, that's good. That's so good, I'm amazed someone besides me came up with it!"

Larry Levine was the funniest kid on the team. Because of this, even though he was a lousy athlete, Larry was very popular with his teammates. He rode the bench most of the time but didn't seem to care much. For him, baseball was all about hanging out with friends and having a few good laughs.

Joey waited until all the others had gone off to get dessert, then sidled over to Larry. "Um, I don't know if I ever mentioned this to you," he said, "but my family's getting this exchange student for a year."

"Oh yeah, I think you said something about that once a long time ago. Like third grade?"

"Yeah, well, it's happening now," Joey told him. "He's coming in a few days. So, like, I'm gonna have to hang around with him a lot, you know, get him used to everything, everybody, like that."

"So, what are you saying?"

"I don't know," Joey said, sighing. "I don't know what I'm saying. It's just . . ."

"What?" Larry asked, his mouth full of chicken salad. "Just spit it out, okay? We've known each other a long time; you can tell me."

"Look, he's like, from this foreign country, okay? Nicaragua or someplace."

"Does he even speak any English?"

"It says so on the papers, but he wrote me this letter, and it was in Spanish."

"So?"

"So, I stink at Spanish."

"You want me to translate?"

"Look, all I'm asking is just, like, don't make fun of him, okay?"

"Me, make fun of somebody?"

"You know how you like to make cracks about people."

25

"Hey, man, if they can't take a joke —"

"No, but this is different, okay? This kid's coming from a foreign country. He doesn't know about anybody or anything, so just . . . take it easy on him, okay? If you don't start, nobody else will."

"How do you know that, dude? It's a free country. People say all kinds of stupid stuff. Whatever comes into their feeble brains, they say it. So don't go blaming me if somebody else rags on him."

"Just don't *you* do it, okay?"

"Okay! Take it easy, dude, it's no biggie."

"You promise?"

"Sure, whatever. So what's this kid's name?"

Joey hesitated. "Hey-SOOS."

"Gesundheit," Larry quipped. "Seriously, his name is WHAT?"

"I told you. Hey-SOOS. It's spelled J-E-S-U-S."

"His name is JESUS?!?" Larry said, doubling over with laughter. "Hey, guys, listen to this!" Before Joey could stop him, Larry was blabbering to whoever could hear him. "Jesus is coming! This is not a drill. Everybody confess your sins!"

"Shut up, Larry!" Joey said, grabbing him by the shirt.

26

"Whoa, watch it," Larry said, removing Joey's hand gingerly. "Just a joke, dude. Gotta have a sense of humor, right?"

"It's not funny," Joey insisted.

"What's he talking about?" Pete asked.

"I've got an exchange student coming to live with me for a year," Joey explained.

"For a whole year?!" Jordan exclaimed. "Man, that's a long time to put up with somebody you don't even know."

Joey secretly agreed, but he didn't let on. He needed his friends to accept Jesus — because if they rejected him, it would mean they were rejecting Joey, too.

"Get this. The kid's name is Jesus!" Larry exclaimed with a laugh.

"Yeah, right," Pete said. "Tell me another one."

"No, it's true!" Larry insisted. "Right, Joey? Isn't that his name?"

"It's Hey-SOOS," Joey corrected him.

"Spanish for 'Jesus,'" Charlie said. "Yeah, I've heard of it. Man, you'd better hope he's not as weird as his name."

"But bring him around, so we can check him out,"

27

Jordan added. "Hey, wouldn't it be funny if his parents were Mary and Joseph?"

They all laughed, except Joey. "That would be Maria and José," Larry corrected them, and everyone laughed again.

Joey walked away, shaking his head. His friends were being idiots, and he didn't like the feeling he was getting. Okay, so most of them had never met a foreign kid before. That was reality in Bordentown. But did they have to be such jerks about it?

Joey pushed open the stairway door so hard that it banged into the wall. What did he care, anyway? Maybe those morons couldn't see it, but being the one kid in town who had a real foreigner living with him was pretty cool. At least that's what he hoped.

At practice that afternoon, he kept thinking about Jesus. Joey figured if he could teach him how to play baseball, it would make it a whole lot easier to fit in. The Bordentown pecking order was mostly determined by athletic ability. *Maybe Jesus is fast,* Joey thought. Then he remembered the photo of the kid with the knobby knees and bowlegs. Not likely.

Joey did some pitching, played some center field,

and took his swings at the plate, but his heart wasn't into practicing. He was still mad at the kids for making fun of Jesus. It was as if they were making fun of *him*. And if they were already starting in, then what was going to happen when Jesus actually arrived?

4

Two days later, on Thursday, another handwritten letter arrived from Jesus. Joey's dad handed it to him, and Joey tore it open and read the translation out loud:

Dearest family,

Warmest greetings from Managua, my city. Here it is hot, and there has been much rain. On the other side of the city, there was a slide of mud and ten houses were broken, with twenty-five people killed. Many times we have disasters here. Hurricanes, earthquakes. Before I was born, my family lost their house in a big earthquake. For two years they lived in a tent before my uncle built them another house, where I live. Here is a picture of me from one year ago at my house where we live now. It is a very nice house I think, but maybe not nice like yours. My uncle says everyone in America is rich.

Joey laughed and, looking at his parents, said, "Yeah, that's us. Rich. Ha."

Joey's dad was a teacher at Bordentown High School, and his mom sold cosmetics to ladies at parties. They were far from rich, like some of the people in town. The Canelos, for instance, had a big mansion up on the hill. And the Alessandras — forget it. Their house was like some big hotel. Pete sometimes had pool parties there, and it was always the big event of the summer.

"We're rich next to most people in the world," his dad said.

"But Jesus's family got up the money to send him here," Joey pointed out. "They must not be too poor."

"Wrong, honey," his mom said. "Most of the money is donated through local church groups and the Community Action Fund here in town. His family only pays a small percentage."

Joey looked at the photo that Jesus had sent. It showed him standing in front of a cement house — more like a box, with windows and a corrugated tin roof. The box looked big enough for about two good-size rooms. Was that Jesus's family's house? Was that what he called big? Did he and his parents and sisters and brothers all live in that little concrete box?

Joey had never thought of himself as rich before. It was a weird feeling. Suddenly he felt embarrassed about showing Jesus their house here in Bordentown. It was huge by comparison — maybe five times bigger.

At the bottom of the photo, Jesus had written his name in bold print: JESUS JAIME RODRIGUEZ. "Jamie?" Joey read. "Hey, his middle name is Jamie!" he said happily. "Jamie" would be an okay thing to call him. No problem there with his friends. Not like introducing him as Jesus, or even Hey-SOOS.

His dad came over to look at the photo. "See — Jamie," Joey pointed out. "Only he spells it weird — J-A-I-M-E."

"Um, that's pronounced 'Hymie,'" his dad informed him.

"Hymie?" Joey repeated, slumping into his chair. "HYMIE?"

Hymie was even worse than Hey-SOOS. "Why can't I just call him Jamie?" Joey asked.

"Because that's not his name, son," his dad said

firmly. "Look, Jesus's being here is not just for him to learn about us. It's for us to learn about him, and his language, and his culture. It's an opportunity for this whole town, not just our family. We ought to take advantage of it."

Of course his dad was right, Joey knew. Still, that didn't solve his problem, or Jesus's, for that matter. "They're gonna make fun of his name, Dad," he said.

"Why don't you let him decide what he wants to be called?" his father suggested. "I'm sure he'll be the best judge of that."

"I'm just trying to help him out."

"Good. You stick to helping him out. Remember that from now on, and as long as he's staying with us, he's your brother. Got it?"

"Yes, Dad," Joey said, sighing. "I've got it. My brother."

Oh, brother, he thought. This had the potential to be a really long, bad year.

Joey and his family spent Saturday morning getting the house ready, especially Sandy's room (his parents were already calling it Jesus's room, but Joey wasn't going to forget his real brother that easily). They fixed up Sandy's old ten-speed bike, too, although Joey wondered whether Jesus even knew how to ride a bike. Did they even *have* bikes in Nicaragua?

That afternoon was the Marlins' next game, against the Cubs, who were 2–2 so far this season. One of the losses was to the Orioles, a team they'd beaten already, so most of the Marlins were going into the game with a lot of confidence. Most — but not Joey.

The game started well, however. In the second inning, he dove and caught a fly ball, then threw out the overeager Cubs runner, who'd tried to advance to third without waiting to see whether Joey caught the ball. That double play ended the inning, and Joey got a lot of mitt slaps on the head and on his behind.

Then, in the third, he hit a bloop fly ball that dropped in between three fielders. Joey wound up on second and scored the game's first run when Charlie Morganstern lined a double to right field. Charlie later scored to make it 2–0, Marlins.

But as he stood out in center during the third inning, Joey started to get nervous. Next inning, and for the rest of the game after that, he'd be pitching. And this time, his whole team was expecting him to succeed. What if he lost his control and couldn't get the ball over the plate? What if he couldn't fool the Cubs hitters the way he'd fooled the Orioles? He knew he didn't have the stuff to blow the ball by anyone — and there was no backup for him if he failed.

"Center field! Center field! Gallagher, wake up!" he suddenly heard Coach Bacino screaming. Joey came out of his trance, looked up, and saw the ball shooting into the outfield between him and Larry Levine, who was playing one of his rare innings in left field.

"You got it! You got it!" Larry yelled, shying away from the hard-hit grounder, lest it bounce up and hit him in the head.

Joey raced to cut the ball off, lunged at the last minute, and snagged it in the webbing of his mitt. He rolled over in a somersault and came up throwing, holding the runner to a single. A whoop went up from the Marlins in the field and on the bench.

But Joey knew he'd turned an easy play into a showboat play by not paying attention. And Coach Bacino knew it, too. He looked at Joey as he came back to the bench when the inning was over, shaking his head as if to say, "I don't know about you, kid."

When he got up to pitch after the Marlins' turn at bat, the score was still 2–0 in his favor. All he had to do was keep the score right where it was. The good thing was, he had an insurance run to work with. No pressure. Not yet.

Not until he walked the first batter he faced. And the second. "Come on!" Pete Alessandra yelled through his catcher's mask. "What are you doing? Throw it in here, man!"

"Come on, Gallagher!" Coach shouted, clapping his hands. He sounded more nervous than reassuring. Joey bit his lower lip and tried to concentrate on Pete's mitt.

He threw a strike right over the middle. The batter just watched it. Obviously the Cubs were going to look for walks until Joey proved he could put the ball over the plate. Joey threw another meatball, and again the batter just stood there. "Stee-rike two!" the umpire yelled.

Now, with two strikes, Joey knew he had the batter where he wanted him. He threw the next pitch high and outside, and the batter swung wildly at it. "Stee-rike three — yer out!" the umpire said, dramatically yanking his fist back to signal his call.

Joey blew out a relieved breath. His heart was pounding so loud he could hear it reverberating in his ears, drowning out the cheers of his teammates. He started the next hitter off with a pitch down low — but it was *too* low, hitting the dirt in front of home plate and bouncing to the backstop over Pete's shoulder. By the time he'd retrieved it, the runners had moved up to second and third. Now a mere single would blow the entire lead.

Joey bore down, staring in at the catcher's mitt. He reared back and threw a slow change-up. The hitter swung early, and Joey was up on the count, 0–1. Next, he fired the ball as hard as he could, aiming shoulder high. The hitter, primed for the slow pitch, swung late.

"Stee-rike two!"

Joey threw his next pitch low and outside. The hitter reached for it and bounced it to the shortstop. Jordan picked it up, and seeing it was too late to prevent the run from coming in, he threw to first for the second out.

Joey fanned the next batter to get out of the inning, but now he only had a one-run lead. Neither team scored in the fifth, with Joey mowing down the bottom of the Cubs order, one-two-three. Still, he wasn't celebrating yet. He knew he'd have to face the Cubs' best hitters in the sixth.

Joey led off at bat at the top of the sixth, determined

to score a run and give himself a bigger cushion. On the first pitch, he smacked a single to right. Then the right fielder bobbled the ball. Joey took off for second and went into a slide as the throw came in. He felt the tag hit his leg just before he touched the bag. "Yer out!" the umpire called.

Joey was disgusted with himself for not making it to second. He threw his batting helmet on the ground, then snatched it back up and trotted off the field.

"Good try, kid," Coach told him as he sat down on the bench. "It was the right play. We need the insurance run."

But they didn't get it, and Joey took the mound with only the slimmest of margins to work with. He knew that if he got the first batter out, it would make things easier and give him the confidence he needed to make it through. So he tried to get ahead of him with a super-slow change-up. Except this time the hitter was ready for it, slapping it over the shortstop's head for a single.

Now the pressure was really on. Joey could feel it twisting his stomach in knots as he tried to concentrate on his next pitch, a fastball. The hitter made contact, barely, and the ball skittered toward second base. Joey reached for it and grabbed it but wasn't sure if he had a play at second or not. He hesitated for an instant, and then it was too late. He turned to first and threw, but the runner was already there.

He didn't hear the moan that went up from the Marlins stands — the pounding in his ears was too loud — but he knew it was there. How could it not be? He'd screwed up badly, making a crucial error at the worst possible time!

He forced himself to concentrate, to shut out everything but the catcher's mitt. The next batter was a huge hulk of a kid, and he was wiggling the bat around like he wanted to hit the ball all the way to China. Joey threw him a trio of slow, tantalizing pitches, some high, some low, and tied him up in knots, striking him out on three pitches.

Next up was the cleanup hitter, and Joey fooled him with a first-pitch fastball right over the plate.

"Come on, Gallagher, you can do it!" Pete yelled from behind his catcher's mask.

Joey reared back and fired a fastball high. The hitter popped it straight up. Pete threw off his mask and tried to get under it. Jordan came in from short, calling for the ball, but it was obvious Pete couldn't hear him, or wasn't listening.

Joey saw that they were going to run into each other. "I got it, I got it!" he cried, and leaped up to grab the ball before the other two collided. But the ball glanced off the webbing of his mitt and skittered off into foul territory.

Joey ran to get it as the runners scooted around the bases. Pete, unhurt thanks to Joey, headed back to the plate to make the play on the first runner coming in. Joey fired it to him, off balance, and Pete caught the ball just as the Cubs runner slid into home. Pete applied the tag — but the runner's cleats knocked the ball out of his mitt!

"Safe!" yelled the umpire, as the ball dribbled toward the mound. Joey got up and ran to get it. The second runner came around third and just kept going. Joey, his eyes on the runner approaching home, reached down to pick up the ball and flip it to Pete — and his hand came up empty!

Another error!

"Safe!" screamed the umpire, as the winning run crossed home.

Cubs 3, Marlins 2. Their first loss of the season — and it was all Joey's fault!

5

Nobody said much as each player gathered up his gear. There was nothing anyone could say that would make the team feel any better. This was a game they should've won. Now that they'd blown it, their record of 4–1 put them in a three-way tie for first place with the Orioles and the Phillies — teams they'd already beaten.

Joey kept his eyes on his shoes. When he finally glanced up, the other kids hurriedly looked away from him. Even Larry Levine was speechless, merely shaking his head in dismay.

The Mighty Marlins were no longer number one, and it hurt. Coach Bacino, hoisting the heavy duffel containing the team's equipment, said, "Look, guys, we'll just have to come back next game and play the way we can play. If we do that, we'll be right there at the end of the season. Don't let one bad loss spoil it for you."

Here's what he didn't say, but what Joey and everyone else knew he wanted to say: "If we'd had Nicky Canelo in there pitching instead of Joey Gallagher, we'd still have a perfect record."

Joey couldn't remember ever feeling this bummed out. He wanted to quit the team, move to another town where nobody knew him, and never see any of these kids again.

Well, maybe that was going too far, he reasoned, calming down a little as he walked toward the station wagon. He could see that both his mom and dad were in the front seat. Great. They'd start off by asking him how the game went, and then, when he told them, they'd gasp and cluck their tongues and say, "Oh, no!" and tell him it would go better next game.

He didn't want to hear any of it. He felt rotten enough already. "We lost," he announced as he threw his bat and mitt into the backseat, sat down with a thud, and slammed the door shut behind him. "And I don't want to talk about it, okay?"

"Whoa," said his mom, glancing over at his dad, who was in the passenger seat.

"Okay, then," his dad said, turning to look at Joey over his shoulder. "Let's forget about the game. Aren't you excited?"

"Excited?"

"About Jesus coming!"

"Oh! Yeah! Right. Sure," Joey said. "Excited. Yeah." In his anguish over losing the game, he'd forgotten they were driving right to the airport afterward. No wonder both his parents had come along to pick him up.

The car was silent for a bit, then his mother said, "I wonder if he'll be bringing cold-weather clothes with him."

"I doubt it, Gail," his dad replied. "They don't have winter there."

"Well, maybe we could let him wear some of Joey's things," she suggested.

"I've gotta share my clothes now?" Joey protested.

"Just the ones you're tired of, son," his dad said. "Come on, now, you've got plenty to spare."

"Whatever," Joey said and slid down low in the backseat, opting out of any further conversation. He wondered what Jesus was going to be like. He knew you couldn't tell — not really — from a photograph

43

and a couple of letters. What if the kid was bratty or weird? What if they had nothing in common and nothing to say to each other? He knew enough to realize that no matter what, his parents would try to push the two of them to be friends. And nothing is harder than making friends when your parents are pushing you to do it. What if Joey hated him?

Or what if Jesus hates me? he suddenly thought. After today, Jesus would have plenty of company. Joey put his headphones on and turned on some music to try to block such thoughts from entering his brain. He bopped his head to the beat so that just in case his parents tried to engage him in conversation, they'd see he couldn't hear them.

After an hour in the car, he heard his mother call out, "We're here!" She made her voice loud enough to penetrate the wall of sound being pumped into his ears through the headphones. "Take that thing off now, Joey. We're going inside."

With a big sigh, Joey took off the headphones and threw them down on the seat, then got out and followed his parents into the terminal.

"Have you got the sign?" his mom asked.

"Right here," his dad said, unfolding a placard that read, WELCOME JESUS!

Oh, brother, thought Joey. *Here we go.* Sure enough, as they stood there holding up their sign and watching people emerge from the customs/baggage-check area, other people gave them lots of space and lots of sidelong glances. "They think we're weird," Joey told his dad.

"Huh? Why in the world would anybody think that?" his mother asked.

"The sign," Joey told her. "They think we're some kind of religious nuts."

She looked at the poster, and it seemed to hit her all of a sudden. "Oh! Well, never mind what anybody thinks. Jesus is his name, after all, honey, and we have to let him know who we are. Remember, he's come all the way here by himself. And we're his new family."

Joey winced. Why did she have to keep putting it that way? Sighing again, he turned his attention back to spotting Jesus. There weren't very many kids by themselves, he noticed. Huh. It was pretty brave of Jesus to come without an escort. Joey didn't think he'd have felt comfortable doing it. Maybe his mom was right, just this once.

Then suddenly, he saw him. A tall, skinny, dark-skinned kid coming through the gate, wearing a white, short-sleeved dress shirt, black dress pants, and sandals. He sort of looked like Jesus in the photo, but Joey wasn't sure. This kid had a shaved head and was at least a foot taller than the one in the photo.

Nevertheless, it was him, all right. When the tall boy looked around as the customs officials checked his bags, he saw the sign. He waved and gave them all a big smile.

"Hey-SOOS!" Joey's mom called out, jumping up and down and clapping her hands. "Oh, darling, isn't this exciting?"

"Sure is," Joey's dad replied, hugging her and waving to Jesus. Joey waved, too, but it was a weak wave, and his smile felt pasted on his face.

Jesus grabbed his bag and his passport and proceeded through the checkpoint.

"Hello! Welcome!" Joey's mom said, giving Jesus a big hug.

"Bienvenido a los Estados Unidos!" his father said in halting Spanish. "Here, let me get those bags for you." He tried to take Jesus's suitcase. At first, Jesus didn't seem to understand and tried to hold tightly to it, but

Joey's dad finally got his point across, saying, "It's all right, it's all right — you're family now. *Familia!*"

"*Sí, familia,*" Jesus echoed, nodding shyly and smiling. He turned to Joey. "You are Ho-ey?" he asked.

"Joey," Joey corrected. "And you're Jesus."

"Jesus, *sí,*" said Jesus. He put out his hand to shake Joey's, and Joey took it. Jesus's hand was sweaty and cool, and his handshake was weak. Joey wiped his hand on his pants when Jesus wasn't looking.

"Come. Our car — our auto — there," Joey's dad said in broken English, pointing to the parking lot. Joey rolled his eyes. Was that how they were all going to talk from now on? For goodness' sake!

"Ah. *Allí?*" Jesus asked.

"*Sí, sí,*" Joey's mom said, although she obviously didn't understand what Jesus had asked.

They walked across the airport parking lot, his parents asking a million questions, such as "How was your flight?" and "Have you eaten dinner?" and "What do you like to eat?"

Jesus did the best he could to answer them, but Joey could tell right away that he didn't speak nearly as much English as they'd said in the letter from the

47

exchange program. He pretty much said *"sí"* or "no," or "good," or "okay," or "no good" to all the questions.

"Mom, he doesn't speak any English at all!" Joey whispered to her while his dad and Jesus put the suitcase and backpack in the trunk.

"Now, honey, maybe he's just shy or tired from his flight," his mom said. That was the end of the discussion, because just then the trunk slammed shut, and everyone got into the car. Jesus sat next to Joey in the back.

"Tu casa — your house — near to airport?" Jesus asked him.

Joey's eyes opened wide. Maybe his mom had been right. It was the most English Jesus had spoken so far. "No. It's far," Joey said.

"Ah. Far. No near." Jesus nodded.

"Yeah, it's about sixty miles . . ." Then he remembered that most countries used the metric system. He did a quick little calculation. "Um, *cien kilómetros.*"

Jesus whistled through his teeth, something Joey had tried for years to do without success. "Nicaragua only *doscientos kilómetros* from *el Atlántico al Pacífico!*" Jesus laughed, holding his hands apart to illustrate.

"Small," Joey said, laughing a little at how Jesus had managed to get his point across.

"America *es más grande, sí?*" Jesus said.

"Oh, yeah," Joey agreed. "Very, very big."

"Hey, CD!" Jesus said, discovering Joey's player and headphones on the seat between them. "Supercool!"

"You know what it is?" Joey asked, surprised.

"*Sí* — yes!" Jesus answered. "Is okay I . . . ?"

"Sure," Joey said. "I don't know if you'll like the music, though."

"I like all kind music," Jesus said. He put on the headphones and started listening. Soon he was bopping his head and laughing. "Supercool. I like very much," he said.

"All right!" Joey said. So far, so good. If Jesus could get into Twisted Fyshburger, Joey had lots more music to turn him on to.

Jesus took off the headphones. "You," he said, offering them to Joey.

"No, that's okay," Joey told him. Jesus put the headphones down on the seat and looked out the window, still bopping his head a little. The sun had set by now. It was getting dark as they got off the interstate and started passing the farmhouses and cornfields that ringed Bordentown.

Ay, mamacita, que casas grandes!" Jesus said, his face glued to the window. "So much *maíz!"*

"Corn, yeah," Joey corrected him.

"You house so much big?"

"Um, not really . . . well, sort of. We're in a town," Joey tried to explain. *"Ciudad pequeño."*

"Ah, *sí — pequeñ*a," Jesus corrected him, laughing a little at Joey's pathetic attempts at Spanish. Then he fell silent and turned to look out the window again. They were coming into Bordentown now, and Joey's mom had taken them in via Borden Avenue, where the town's biggest mansions were.

Joey felt himself getting angry. Why was she doing that? Couldn't she see that Jesus was already gawking, even at ordinary houses? Was she trying to make him feel bad about his own house back home or what? He wished she would use her head sometimes, but there wasn't much he could do about it at the moment.

"In Nicaragua, only rich, rich people have such house," Jesus said.

"Uh-huh," Joey said, a little embarrassed. "The

50

people on this street are pretty rich, actually. But . . . but I'm sure Nicaragua is nice, too," he offered.

"Oh, *sí*. Some place nice, some no nice," Jesus replied. "Where I live nice, but no like this."

"You're much taller than your picture, Jesus," Joey's mom said from the front seat.

"*Qué?*"

"*Más grande*," Joey translated, realizing that his Spanish was not even as good as Jesus's pathetic English.

"*Yo? O, sí!* Since one year, I am grow *catorce centímetros*. Fourteen. Now my clothes, everything too small!"

"Well, don't worry," Joey's mom assured him. "There's always the mall. We can help you find some new clothes tomorrow. Joey's sure won't fit you."

"Mall? What is mall?" Jesus asked.

"Wait till you see it," Joey's dad said. "*Muchas bodegas*."

Joey rolled his eyes. He was sure his dad hadn't said it right, but he didn't know how to improve on it. "*Mercado*," he tried.

"*Mercado grande, sí?*"

"Yes. *Sí. Mercado grande*."

51

As they turned onto their street, Cherry Tree Lane, Jesus kept whistling at all the beautiful houses. It was dark now, and on either side homes were lit up from inside, as families sat down to dinner. *"Ay, que bonitas!"* Jesus said, almost in a whisper. "America very much beautiful! I like."

"Muchas gracias!" Joey's dad said.

"And we like *you*, Jesus," his mom added, making Joey cringe with embarrassment.

"Gracias," Jesus said, and although it was dark in the car, Joey knew he must be blushing.

They pulled into the driveway and got out. Jesus was staring at the house — a four-bedroom colonial with a large front yard — like he'd just been transported to another planet. *"Caramba!"* he said under his breath. "You very, very rich!"

Joey wanted to protest that they weren't rich at all, only middle class. But he knew he could never convince Jesus. "Come on in," he told him, and led Jesus inside as his parents grabbed the suitcase and knapsack. "I'll show you around the place."

Jesus seemed stunned. *"Tantos cuartos!"* he kept saying. "So much rooms only for three people!"

"Well, we used to be four," Joey explained. "My

brother, Sandy, is away at college — I mean, *universidad.*"

"Ah, *sí,*" Jesus said. "So many *cuartos!*" He kept staring at everything — the couches, the rugs, the kitchen appliances, and then, upstairs, the bedrooms and — "So many *cuartos de baño!* One, two, three . . ."

"Two and a half," Joey said, but Jesus didn't seem to get the distinction. "One doesn't have a bath. Anyway, let me show you your room. It's actually my brother, Sandy's, room, but —"

"Each one have room only for to sleep," Jesus mumbled in disbelief. *"Ay, muchacho,* you are so lucky."

"Well hey," Joey said, not knowing how to respond. "Now you're lucky, too." He'd always thought of his life as happy and good. But until this moment, it had really never hit him how rich he was — how rich almost everyone he knew was, compared with many people in the rest of the world.

Jesus sat down on Sandy's bed and looked around at his new digs. "Bed nice!" he said, bouncing up and down on it a little. "Soft. Sleep good." He yawned suddenly and leaned back, his arms spread out as he collapsed on the bed.

"Yeah," Joey said with a laugh. "You're probably

wiped out from the long trip, huh? You want to go to sleep?"

"Oh, no now!" Jesus said, springing up again and reaching for his backpack. He dug his hand into one of the outer pockets and drew something out. "For you . . . Joey," he said, shyly offering it to him.

Joey took the object and looked at it closely. It was a tiny box, so small it fit in the palm of his hand. It seemed to be woven of strands of reed or wicker or something, and the top was red silk. "You open now," Jesus said, his eyes flickering with happiness.

Joey opened the box. Inside was a string of tiny dolls, woven together in a line by their hips. Each figure was distinct — some tall, some short, some male, some female. "Wow," he said. "Thanks. But, what is it?"

"I make myself," Jesus said. "Is *familia* . . . family."

Joey looked at the new arrival. Maybe Jesus wasn't really his brother. Maybe he never would be. But Joey already felt like they were family somehow, in a different kind of way. "Thanks, Jesus," he said again. "It's . . . it's supercool, dude."

"Gimme five!" Jesus said. And Joey, taken totally by surprise, did just that.

6

Jesus slept late the next day. By the time he showered (for half an hour!), came downstairs, and ate breakfast, it was almost 1:00. Time to go to the mall.

Joey was glad to be going. For one thing, it would give him a chance to get Jesus used to life in the United States before he actually went to school and met everyone. There were only two weeks left in the school year, but Jesus would be going along with Joey just to get his feet wet. That way, when he went in September, as a real student, it wouldn't be total culture shock for him.

Jesus clearly was making progress with his English already. He seemed less shy than the night before, more willing to risk making a mistake in English and be corrected for it. "You tell me if I say wrong word, *sí?*" he begged Joey.

Well, sure, but he made about three mistakes every time he opened his mouth. Joey wasn't about to correct them all at once. They'd never get anywhere that way! Little by little, though, he pointed out the right way to say things. Joey could only imagine how *he'd* have felt if the shoe had been on the other foot — if he'd been visiting Jesus's family in Nicaragua, trying to make himself understood in Spanish — *sheesh!*

There was another reason Joey was happy to be going to the mall today. He'd been embarrassed the night before, when he didn't have any present to give Jesus in return for the beautiful woven box with the tiny family in it. Joey didn't know if the family was supposed to be him and his parents, or Jesus's family, or just some symbolic one. Jesus had told him it was for "good luck," and he'd used a name for them, but Joey couldn't remember it.

Anyway, it was a beautiful gift, and Joey had had nothing to give in return. Well, today he'd fix that. His birthday was only a month away, and his parents always gave him some cash as a gift. He'd just ask for it in advance, so he could buy something for his "new brother."

He pulled his dad aside while his mom was in a

clothing store, getting Jesus some jeans. "Dad, can I have fifty bucks for my birthday in advance?" he asked.

"Huh? Your birthday's not till —"

"I know when it is, Dad. I just want to get Jesus something."

"Well, what did you have in mind, son?"

"I don't know. Something good. I'll know it when I see it."

"Well, all right, but don't expect anything on July fifteenth."

"I won't. Thanks!" Joey said, taking the money and running off.

"Hey, where are you going?" his dad called after him.

"I'll meet you at the food court in half an hour!" he answered, shouting back over his shoulder as he ran. He hadn't gone far when he saw the perfect gift in the display window of a sporting-goods store. It was a baseball mitt. "Sweet!" Joey said, a smile breaking out on his face.

He'd been thinking of giving Jesus one of his CD players. He had two, after all. But giving Jesus his old stuff didn't make it. It wasn't the same kind of gift Jesus had given him.

A baseball mitt, on the other hand . . .

Either Jesus had played baseball before, in which case a new mitt was a cool gift, no doubt — "super-cool," as Jesus liked to say — or he'd never played ball before, in which case it couldn't hurt to get him started. There was no better way to be down with Joey's friends than playing ball with them.

He picked out a nice mitt — big pocket, soft, deep brown leather — for forty-five dollars. On sale, Joey noted with satisfaction — original price: seventy dollars. What a bargain! It was even better than his own mitt. Joey didn't feel jealous, though. He wanted to give Jesus something really great.

He met the others back at the food court and quickly hid the bag with the mitt inside one of the larger shopping bags. They ate dinner out that night, so it wasn't until almost bedtime that Joey knocked on Jesus's door.

"*Sí?* Come in."

"Hi, it's me," Joey said, holding the mitt behind his back.

"*Hola, amigo,*" Jesus greeted him. "Gimme five!"

"Where'd you get that, anyway — that 'gimme five' stuff?"

"We see American TV show sometimes."

"Huh," Joey said, wondering what shows they watched. "I'm surprised you never saw a mall. Anyway, I've got something for you, dude. Here." Joey thrust the mitt at Jesus. "It's a present."

He watched as Jesus stared at the mitt, then slowly, ever so slowly, reached out and took it in his hands. *"Madre de Dios . . ."* he breathed. *"Béisbol!"*

So he does know what it is, Joey thought, relieved. Apparently Jesus was pleased with the gift. "Overwhelmed" was actually more like it.

"Gracias . . ." he mumbled, his lower lip trembling as a lone tear trickled its way down his cheek. *"Gracias."* Stroking the soft leather as if it were gold, Jesus slowly put his hand into the mitt — his right hand. The *wrong* hand.

Oh, brother, thought Joey. Teaching Jesus to play baseball was going to be a real project. "Not like that," he said. "Here, let me show you." He removed the mitt slowly from Jesus's right hand and slipped it onto his left hand.

Jesus looked down at the floor, tears still dripping down off his chin.

"Listen," Joey told him, "I'm sorry if I did something wrong . . ."

"No . . . is no that," Jesus said in a voice barely louder than a whisper.

"Then what?"

Jesus bit his lower lip. "Is nothing," he said. "Is beautiful present. Much more better than my present to you."

"Oh, is that it?" Joey said, embarrassed. "Forget it. Hey, man, I liked your present a lot. And you made it yourself. I just went and bought this. No big deal."

"No big deal?" Jesus repeated. "For me is big deal. Thank you, Joey. Is best present I ever get."

"Cool. So you want to throw the ball around outside?" he asked.

"Oh. No. No right now. Is . . . is nighttime."

"We could flip on the driveway lights. My friends and I do it all the time."

"No . . . no thanks you," Jesus said, caressing the glove like it was a newborn puppy. "I . . . *mañana,* maybe. Tomorrow."

"Okay then," Joey said, giving up for the moment. "Tomorrow. After school."

"Ah . . . *escuela,*" Jesus remembered. "I just to go around with you, *sí?*"

"Yeah, that's right," Joey reassured him. "Don't

worry about it. You don't have to do the work or anything. Not till September, and you'll be fine by then. I mean, your English will be fine."

"I go with you to class?" Jesus asked, still seeming scared.

"Yup. The whole day. Don't worry about a thing, dude. You're going to be fine. Supercool."

"*Sí*," Jesus said, smiling broadly. "Supercool."

"That's right — gimme five, man."

"*Sí!* Gimme five!" And Jesus did.

7

"Good morning, class," Mrs. Shepard said. She had a voice that could cut through noise like a buzz saw. Everyone fell silent almost at once. Joey had pulled an extra chair next to his desk for Jesus. "I want to introduce you all to a new arrival — Jesus Rodriguez."

Oh, no, Joey thought. She'd pronounced it "GEE-zuz." Sure enough, the class erupted in titters. "Um, Mrs. Shepard?" he said, raising his hand.

"Don't interrupt, Joey — you'll have a chance when I'm finished. Now, Jesus is visiting from Managua, Nicaragua. Can anyone tell me where that is?"

Andy Norton, the self-appointed home-run king and all-around smart aleck, shot his hand up. "Um, Israel?"

More laughter from the class. "That will do," Mrs. Shepard said with a scowl. "Yes, Brianne?"

"It's in Central America."

"Thank you, Brianne," Mrs. Shepard said with a smile. "Yes, Central America. And what language do they speak there? Damon?"

"Spanish."

"Very good. Now, Jesus is here for a whole year, as an exchange student. He's going to be living with Joey Gallagher's family, and next year, he's going to be taking classes with all of you. So I hope you'll all give our guest a nice, warm Bordentown welcome."

That was the signal for the class to applaud, and they did. But as the clapping began to subside, Joey heard someone behind him say, "Maybe we can get him to walk on water." Laughter followed, and Joey was glad Jesus's English wasn't good enough for him to understand the joke.

"Does anyone have any questions for Jesus?" Mrs. Shepard continued. Joey lowered his face into his hands. He knew what was coming next.

"Yes," Andy said. "Jesus, how do I get into heaven?"

The whole class erupted in howls of laughter.

"That will do!" Mrs. Shepard's angry voice boomed. "Mr. Norton, apologize to Jesus right now."

"Yes, ma'am," Andy said, trying but failing to stifle the urge to giggle. "I'm sorry, Jesus. Forgive me."

Turning his back to the teacher for a moment, Andy crossed himself. Naturally, this provoked another round of hilarity.

Joey could feel the blood rising to his face. He glanced at Jesus, who looked horribly uncomfortable. "Hey!" Joey said, standing up. "His name's not Jesus, okay? It's Hey-SOOS."

This only poured gasoline on the fire. "Hey-SOOOOOS!" one of the boys bellowed. And soon, the whole class was doing it. Only Mrs. Shepard's voice, and the smack of the ruler on her desk, brought the insanity to a halt.

"All right, that's quite enough," she said. "This whole class will be reported to the principal for bad behavior. And I'm sorry, Jesus, for mispronouncing your name. Welcome to Bordentown. We really are not bad people here — even though some of us behave badly on occasion."

She gave a hard glance around the room. "And now, please open your history textbooks to page one sixty-seven — the voyages of Christopher Columbus."

The rest of the morning was pretty normal. Every once in a while, Joey would catch someone staring at them or hear a brief, stifled giggle in back of them. He kept checking Jesus out to see how he was reacting. But Jesus was keeping his feelings to himself. Joey hadn't seen him this quiet since they'd first picked him up at the airport.

At lunchtime, after they got their food, Larry Levine came over to sit with them. *"Qué pasa, amigo?"* he said, shaking Jesus's hand. The two of them started speaking in Spanish — so fast that Joey could barely understand half of what they were saying. Larry was a whiz in Spanish class, and his parents had a condo in Cancún, Mexico, so he got to practice his Spanish every winter break.

Joey knew enough Spanish to understand that Larry was asking Jesus how he liked the United States — and Bordentown in particular. Jesus was saying he liked it, how beautiful it was, how rich. Then Larry asked him about Nicaragua. As Jesus started describing it in rapid-fire Spanish, Joey realized that Jesus was feeling homesick.

Joey was glad that Larry seemed to be over making fun of Jesus's name. In fact, he was being really friendly to Jesus. Joey only hoped other kids would do the same.

Brianne Nabors came over to sit with them and joined in the conversation in Spanish. Brianne was a real brain. Joey secretly thought she was the nicest and prettiest girl in his class. He could tell she was truly interested in getting to know Jesus. He wasn't sure if she was just being nice or if she wanted to meet someone from a different country.

Joey was glad Jesus was making friends, even though he did feel a little left out of the conversation. He knew his Spanish wasn't good enough. He sat back and ate his chocolate pudding, thinking about how much better his Spanish would get with Jesus to help him.

Then he saw Andy Norton, Damon Krupp, and Chris O'Brien making their way toward them.

"Hi!" Damon said. "How're you doin', Jesus?" He pronounced it "GEE-zuz." Joey winced. Why did some people have to be such jerks?

"Is your mom's name Mary?" Chris asked, provoking sniggers from Andy and Damon.

"Why don't you get lost, okay?" Joey heard himself say. He couldn't believe he'd uttered the words!

"Whoa!" Damon said, wheeling on him. "What did you just say?"

"You heard me," Joey shot back. "Get lost if you can't be a decent human being."

Everyone at the surrounding tables grew suddenly quiet. Damon narrowed his eyes, grabbed Joey by the shirt, and dragged him to a standing position.

"Careful, Damon," Brianne said, standing up. "You get caught beating someone up, you get suspended, you know."

Coming from Brianne, this had the effect of throwing a bucket of ice over the trio of brutes. Damon released his hold on Joey, muttering. "I'll let it go this time." Then he picked up Larry's dish of chocolate pudding and slowly dumped it on Joey's shirt. "Oops. Sorry. Clumsy me."

The threesome guffawed as they walked away. Joey stood there in shock, watching the pudding slide down his shirt and onto the floor.

"You'd better go wash your shirt before it stains," Larry advised him.

"It's too late," Brianne said. "That'll never come out. Oooh, I hate those losers! Sorry, Jesus —" (she pronounced it perfectly, Joey noted) "— I guess there are a few bad apples in every barrel."

"*Qué?*" Jesus asked, confused.

"We're not all stupid, like those guys," Larry said.

"I guess I'll go clean up," Joey said, feeling miserable about everything — about his shirt, about the near fight, and especially about how Jesus must be feeling. Although Jesus didn't show it, Joey knew it couldn't feel very good to be made fun of and to see your new friend suffer for your sake.

As he got up to go, Brianne rose from her seat and came over to him. "I think you were fantastic," she said softly, and leaning in, she kissed him on the cheek.

Joey stopped breathing. He felt like he was going to explode. He'd never been kissed like that before, and by someone he really liked, too! It almost made the whole nightmare scene worth it. As he walked to the bathroom to wash off, he had a new spring in his step.

After school, when they were home and hanging out in Jesus's room, Joey asked him what he'd thought about school that day.

Jesus looked at him with sad eyes. "I think those boys no like me," he said.

Joey shook his head. "It isn't that," he said. "It's just, most of the kids around here have never met anyone

68

from another country before. Someone who speaks a different language and has a weird name."

Jesus shrank back. "My name no good?" he asked, horrified. "But is name of *Cristo!* How no good?"

"It's just, in the United States, we don't name kids after Jesus. It's just not done."

"In my country, many, many boys name Jesus."

"I realize that. But here . . ."

"You want I change my name?" Jesus asked.

"No! No, no, of course not!" Joey said, too quickly. "Well, maybe, while you're here, you might want to go by something else. You know, like a tag."

"Tag? What is tag?"

"Like a nickname."

"No *comprendo.*"

"Like me, for instance. They sometimes call me Junior, 'cause my dad's name is Joe, too."

Jesus clearly didn't get it.

"Like, your middle name is Jaime, right?" He pronounced it "Hymie."

"*Sí.* Jaime. I be Jaime in America?"

"Mmm, maybe not Hymie. But you know what? Here, we pronounce Hymie 'Jamie.' That'd be an okay name."

"Jamie? Is strange name. I never hear before."

"Anyway, think about it. It's totally up to you, okay? You don't have to change anything if you don't want to. Forget I even said anything. It's those morons who have to change, not you."

"Moron?"

"And don't ever call them that, okay? It's not a nice word."

"Okay," Jesus said. "I no say nothing." And the two boys shared a laugh.

"Hey, want to play catch outside?" Joey asked. "Break in your new mitt?"

"I . . . I think maybe later," Jesus said, looking uncomfortable.

"Aw, come on, you might as well get started. I've got a ball game after school tomorrow, and you can warm me up before I come in to pitch. Come on, let's go." Unwilling to take no for an answer, he grabbed Jesus by the arm and led him outside.

Again, Jesus tried to put the mitt on the wrong hand. "No, like this," Joey corrected him, putting it on his left hand. "There you go. Now, I'm going to throw you the ball, and you throw it back, okay?"

"*Sí,*" said Jesus, still looking like he wanted to be someplace else.

Joey threw him the ball. Jesus caught it fine — two-handed, but at least he didn't drop it. Then he took the ball and tried to throw it back. But his throw was awful. Pathetic. Jesus threw like a little girl, putting the wrong foot forward and pushing the ball out of his palm, like it was sticky and disgusting.

Joey sighed and picked up the ball. "Try again," he said. "You'll get used to it." He threw it to Jesus, who again caught it just fine. The second throw, though, was even worse. It went straight up in the air and landed at Jesus's feet.

"Maybe we try again *mañana,*" he suggested.

"No way," Joey insisted. "You've got to get used to it, that's all."

"Oh," said Jesus.

"What's the matter, don't you like baseball?" Joey asked. "You seemed so happy to get the mitt."

"Oh, yes, very happy!" Jesus assured him. "Please. I love *béisbol* very much. Let us play more. I get used to, soon, maybe."

"Okay then," Joey said. "Let's keep practicing."

The two of them kept at it till Joey's mom and dad called them in for dinner. But Jesus's throwing didn't get any better. Not at all. Jesus had said he loved baseball, but it looked to Joey like he hadn't played much in the past. He sure wasn't very good in the present. And his future in the game, as far as Joey could see, was strictly as a fan.

8

I no like be Jamie." Fourth period had just ended, and they were on their way to the cafeteria for lunch.

The statement caught Joey by surprise. "How come?"

"Jamie is name for girl."

"Well, but —"

"Jamie in history class, she is girl, no?"

"Yeah, but it's for both —"

"I no be Jamie," Jesus said, blushing. "No way, José."

"Hey, we say that, too!" Joey said, surprised again.

"Say what?"

"'No way, José.' It's an American expression."

"No, is Nicaraguan."

"Whatever," Joey said, shrugging.

"So, I no Jamie, okay? Jesus my name."

73

"Okay, okay," Joey said, trying to keep his annoyance from showing. "Like I said, dude, whatever."

If there were any hard feelings, they vanished after school, when Joey's mom presented Jesus with Sandy's old bike. Of course, it didn't look old. She'd had it all fixed up and repainted at the bicycle store, and tied it up with a big red ribbon on the handlebars. Jesus let out a yell of sheer joy and ran straight for it. *"Qué fantástico!"* he said in a hoarse voice, as tears trickled down his cheeks.

"Do you know how to ride?" Joey asked.

"Oh, *sí*," Jesus said excitedly. "I have once bicycle, but no like this!"

"Word?" Joey said. "Hey, cool. We can ride over to the field for the game."

"Not before you have something to eat," his mom said, going inside.

"Tan bueno!" Jesus whispered, running his hand slowly over the bike. "I never have something so beautiful." Then he saw the gearshift. *"Qué es?"* he asked Joey.

"What? The gears?"

"Gears? What is 'gears'?"

Joey winced. "Okay," he said. "I guess your bike didn't have gears. Well, they make the bike go faster or slower."

"No make with feet?" Jesus asked, surprised.

"No. I mean, yeah, of course you make with feet. I mean, you pedal it, but the gears — oh, skip it. Just put it in fifth gear and leave it there for now."

Jesus looked confused. Joey put a hand on his shoulder and said, "Come on inside and let's eat. You'll figure it out eventually."

After eating their snack and changing, Joey and Jesus rode their bikes over to the baseball field. Today, the Marlins were playing the lowly 0–5 Dodgers. This game promised to be a piece of cake, with or without Nicky Canelo.

Nicky was sitting in the stands when Joey and Jesus got there. Joey made the introductions. "What up, Jesus?" Nicky said, pronouncing it perfectly and with no hint of amusement. *"Cómo estás?"*

"Estoy bien!" Jesus replied with a big smile.

"I'd shake your hand, but . . ." Nicky held up his right hand, with its soft cast and sling.

"Ay, de mi!" Jesus breathed. "You break?"

"Nah," Nicky said, shaking his head. "I'll be okay pretty soon. I can't stand sitting here watching."

"Me also," Jesus said. Joey shook his head and stifled the urge to laugh. For a kid who could barely throw the ball, Jesus sure talked a good game.

Jesus and Nicky plopped down together side by side in the bleachers, and Joey went down to the bench to join the rest of the Marlins. Out on the field, the Dodgers were already warming up. Their pitcher was whizzing it in there pretty good. Still, Joey felt sure he could get a couple of hits today. After all, the Dodgers hadn't won a game yet.

Penciled into the leadoff spot, Joey stepped into the batter's box to start the game. The pitcher threw and Joey took the pitch, sizing up its speed and movement. The next pitch looked high, but it was called a strike, too. "What?" Joey said.

"Play ball," the umpire warned. Joey stifled his urge to argue and got back in the batter's box. The pitcher wound and threw. Joey swung . . . and whiffed. "Steerike three! Yer out!" the umpire called, a little too eagerly, it seemed to Joey.

The next two batters managed only weak pop-ups,

and the inning was over. Jesus kept cheering loudly from the sidelines, but most of it was in Spanish, and even the English part was hard to understand.

Still, Joey got the idea. He wanted to do well for Jesus, to show what a good ballplayer he was, but he sure hadn't started out very well. On his way to the outfield, he asked Jordan Halpin what was up with the pitcher. "He's new," Jordan said. "This is his first game. Just moved here from Gordonhurst."

"He's good."

"Yeah, well, don't worry, we'll get to him. I'm up next inning, man. No prob." Jordan Halpin had plenty of confidence, and with good reason. He'd been an all-star since fourth grade.

Joey spent the first three innings in the outfield, but nothing came his way. The Dodgers were pathetic hitters — except for the new kid, who laced a solo home run to left field in the second inning. Going into the fourth, it was 1–0, Dodgers, because the mighty Marlins hadn't gotten a single runner on base!

Joey led off the fourth inning. He'd already struck out once, but this time he was facing a different pitcher. This one threw it so slow that Joey got over-anxious and tried to hit the ball out of the park. He whiffed on two straight pitches before finally making contact, hitting a dribbler up the third-base line.

Joey ran for all he was worth, trying to leg it out for a single. But the Dodgers catcher made a good play on the ball and threw him out by a step. Joey slammed his helmet on the ground in disgust. The umpire warned Coach Bacino that one more outburst from Joey would get him tossed from the game.

The coach grabbed Joey in the dugout and asked, "What's with you today? Are you gonna settle down or what? Because I'll get somebody else to pitch if you're so out of control."

Before Joey could reply, there was a big cheer. Pete Alessandra had hit a long shot over the center fielder's head. He rounded the bases for a game-tying homer.

"Don't worry, Coach, I'm okay," Joey said, determined to do on the mound what he hadn't been able to do at the plate — help his team win a game.

He started by getting the first two Dodgers to hit grounders, then got a strikeout to end the fourth inning. In the fifth, the Marlins went ahead on two errors and a double by Charlie Morganstern. The score was now 2–1, Marlins, and Joey knew his job was to hold the Dodgers scoreless over the next two innings.

He got the bottom of their order out in the fifth, sitting them down with only an infield single. The Marlins came close to scoring in their half of the sixth, but Joey popped up to end the threat. He was so angry at himself that he nearly threw the bat. At the last minute, he remembered the umpire's warning and held on to it until he came back to the bench to get his mitt.

"No walks!" Coach Bacino told him.

"No walks," Joey echoed as he took the mound again.

The first batter bunted Joey's fastball down the third-base line. Joey fielded the ball but slipped as he threw to first, and the ball sailed high. When the right fielder finally threw it back in from foul territory, the runner was already at third base.

Joey really had to buckle down now, or the score would be tied. Starting the next batter off with a change-up, he got him to pop up to first. One away, two to go.

Joey got two strikes on the next hitter, then threw a wild pitch that hit him in the helmet. A gasp went up from the crowd, but luckily, the Dodger hitter wasn't hurt. Still, the whole thing shook Joey up. Now there were runners at first and third, with only one out. The whole game was on the line.

"Keep it low!" Coach Bacino yelled. "Look for two!"

"Double play!" Jesus yelled from the sidelines. Joey looked over at him. So, Jesus *did* know something about the game after all! Well, Joey was going to give them a double play, all right. He fired a fastball, outside and at the knees. The batter swung at the pitch and sent a grounder to the shortstop. Jordan picked it up and flicked a quick toss to second, where the second baseman grabbed it, stepped on the bag, and fired to first for the game-ending double play!

The Marlins whooped it up as they ran to the bench, but they were obviously more relieved than anything else. They'd played the worst team in the league, and they'd almost blown the game!

"You pitch *fantástico!*" Jesus congratulated him. But Joey shook his head in disgust.

"I played terrible," he said. "I almost lost the game for us with that error. And oh-for-three? Gimme a break! I *never* do that!"

Joey felt embarrassed. He'd wanted so much to impress Jesus that he'd tried too hard and made a total fool of himself instead.

"I like pitch, too!" Jesus said enthusiastically.

"Uh, yeah," Joey said, trying to sound convincing. "Right."

Jesus caught the false note in his voice and looked at the ground. "Maybe I practice more. I get better," he said softly.

"Come on," Joey said, grabbing him by the arm and leading him toward the bike rack. "Let's go home. We'll throw it around in the driveway after dinner tonight."

"You boys have a good time?" Joey's mom asked when they got home.

"*Sí,*" Jesus said. "Joey *jugó estupendamente!*"

"Cut it out," Joey told him. "I stunk up the joint," he said to his mother.

"He make for double play to save game!" Jesus argued.

"I couldn't hit to save my life. I nearly blew the whole thing with an error —"

"Whoa, whoa!" his mom said. "Listen, it was a simple question. I'm not looking for the whole play-by-play. Jesus, tonight Mr. Gallagher and I are going to a retirement dinner for someone in his office. I made you boys London broil. It's in a covered pan in the fridge, so Joey, just heat it up whenever you're hungry, okay? Salad's in the big bowl, mashed potatoes are all cooked — stick them in the microwave for a couple minutes . . ." Having given them their instructions, she left the house, got in the station wagon, and drove away.

Joey was proud that his parents trusted him. They knew he was old enough and mature enough to take care of himself and Jesus for the evening. But Jesus didn't seem to think it was so remarkable that they were going to fend for themselves. "You know how to cook?" Joey asked him.

"Oh, *sí*. I cook for my family many times. Enchiladas, *huevos rancheros*, tortillas . . ."

"Can you do fajitas?"

"*Sí*, the best! But your mother say she make food already, no?"

"Yeah, I guess London broil's pretty good."

"What is 'London broil'?"

"Steak, sliced, on toast."

"Steak! *Que bueno!* Here you have meat every day?"

"Well, not really. We have fish and chicken sometimes . . ."

82

"Is meat, no?"

"No. Well, yeah, sort of, but — never mind. Listen, I'm sticking this in the oven for a few minutes. I've got to go do my homework. It'll be ready by the time I'm done. I'll see you later, okay?"

"Okay."

As Jesus picked up the remote and flicked on the kitchen TV, Joey hoisted his book bag over his shoulder and climbed the stairs to his bedroom.

Soon, he was done. He came downstairs, ready to finish making dinner. He found Jesus sitting at the kitchen table with scissors, cutting up a cardboard cereal box.

Hmmm . . . weird. Joey hung back, watching, as Jesus cut the box and folded it . . . into a crude baseball mitt!

Joey entered the room, and Jesus looked up sharply, as if he'd been caught doing something he shouldn't. "You making a mitt?" Joey asked.

Jesus nodded. *"S-sí,"* he said. "Is kind I have in Nicaragua."

"This is what you play ball with?" Joey asked, amazed. No wonder Jesus had cried when he'd given him the new leather mitt!

In fact, Jesus looked like he was choking up now. "I go . . . write letter to my family back home," he said and left the room.

Joey picked up the pathetic excuse for a mitt and tried it on his hand. "I couldn't catch a cold with this thing," he said to himself. "Maybe that's why Jesus is having such a hard time with a real mitt."

He followed Jesus into the rec room, where he'd flopped down on the couch and was watching a baseball game on TV. "I thought you were going to write a letter," Joey said, plopping down beside him.

"Maybe later," Jesus said, distracted. "You see this guy? He from my country!" He pointed to Enrique Velandia, a lefty slugger for the visiting team. "He is *el mejor!*"

"MVP?"

"*Sí*, MVP in all Nicaragua."

"Wow." Joey watched Velandia hit a triple to deep center. "Yeah, he's pretty good all right." But the thing that interested him more was Jesus's apparent knowledge of the game. For a kid who couldn't play to save his life, he sure knew a lot about baseball — or *béisbol*, as he called it.

"I'm gonna go finish making our steak," Joey said, getting up and going into the kitchen. He followed his mom's instructions as far as he could remember them and even added easy-bake dinner rolls for good measure. He set the table with forks, knives, napkins — the works. "Food's ready!" he called.

"Un minuto!" Jesus shouted back. "Is two out, base loaded!"

Joey shook his head, surprised yet again by how devoted Jesus seemed to the game. Something was definitely wrong with this picture. He'd never seen a total nonathlete so into a sport.

Jesus gave a shout of joy — "Yesss!" — and came bounding into the kitchen. "Grand slam!"

"Hey, I root for the home team, yo."

"Oh. *Sí,* sorry. I for Velandia."

"It's okay. I don't care. Come on, dig in. Food's ready."

Jesus sat down and grabbed his fork and knife. He began sawing at the steak, shoving forkfuls into his mouth. "Mmmm!" he said, nodding appreciatively. *"Delicioso!"*

"Thanks," Joey said, laughing. And then it hit him.

There was something strange about the way Jesus was holding his fork and knife. Joey looked at his own hands, then back at Jesus's. He was holding the utensils in the wrong hands . . .

Joey grabbed a dinner roll. "Jesus — heads up!" he said, tossing it quickly at him. With lightning reflexes, Jesus reached up and caught it cleanly — in his left hand!

"Jesus — you're a *lefty?*" Joey gasped.

Jesus looked down at his plate and nodded sadly.

No wonder he couldn't throw the ball to save his life! Joey thought. *I couldn't either, with my left hand.* No wonder he'd tried to put the mitt on his right hand when he first got it. And no wonder Joey couldn't make the cardboard mitt fit his left hand!

"Why didn't you say something, man?"

"You spend so much money. I . . . I no want tell you is no good for me."

"Hey, we can return it, no problem. We'll just get you a lefty mitt."

Jesus seemed stunned. "*Verdad?*" he asked.

"Totally," Joey assured him.

Jesus got up and hugged him. "I never know they

make for lefties. I think is only for much money, for professional, no?"

"Of course not!" Joey insisted. "Don't worry about it, Jesus." He shook his head in amazement. "I'll bet you're a lot better when you play left-handed, huh?"

"*Sí*," said Jesus, smiling shyly. "A little."

Joey wondered just how much better. One thing was for sure — Jesus was turning out to be full of surprises.

9

As they left school the next day, Joey and Jesus headed straight for the curb, where Joey's mom was waiting for them in the wagon. "Got it?" Joey asked her.

She gave him a thumbs-up. "It's in the backseat. Check it out." Joey got in. Jesus, who had gone around to the other side, already had the glove on and was beaming a smile that could have lit up the whole world.

"*Sí! Que lindo!* How beautiful . . ."

"Now don't go crying about it again," Joey told him. "It's really no big deal. See, in America, stores make exchanges all the time."

"You no understand," Jesus told him. "I no can explain." And that's all he would say. Jesus just sat there, caressing the soft leather, pounding the pocket, making the mitt his very own.

They reached the field, and Joey led Jesus over to Coach Bacino. "Hey, Coach?" he said. "Is it okay if my friend Jesus works out with us?"

Coach Bacino looked Jesus up and down. "Lefty, huh?"

"*Sí,*" said Jesus, smiling that goofy grin of his.

"You ever play before?"

"*Sí, sí! Mucho béisbol.*"

"Okay, get out in center field. Let's see how you look."

Jesus ran out to center so fast that even Joey was surprised. "Well, he sure can run," Coach Bacino said, chuckling. "Let's see what he does with this." He hit a line drive. Jesus streaked after the ball the second it was hit, ran it down, and snared it in the webbing of his mitt. Then he spun around and fired a perfect strike to second base.

"Wow!" Coach Bacino gasped as the whole team erupted in applause.

"Hey, who's that?" Jordan asked.

"It's that Mexican kid," Ellis Suggs said. "The one who lives with Gallagher."

"His name's Jesus, you believe it?" Charlie said, and everyone laughed.

"Hey, shut up," Joey blurted out. "There's nothing wrong with his name, okay? Just get over it."

"Shut up yourself, Gallagher," Charlie shot back. "It's a free country."

"It's not free of jerks, obviously," Joey said.

"What'd you call me?"

"Nothing. Did I say you?"

"I'm not stupid. I know what you meant."

"So why are you asking me?" By this time, Joey and Charlie were nose to nose, and Coach Bacino had to step in to break it up.

"What do you think you're doing?" he yelled. "We're supposed to be on the same team, okay? If you can't say something positive, then keep it zipped. Next one who mouths off rides the bench — and I'm not kidding!"

The team settled back down. Coach Bacino hit another screamer Jesus's way. Jesus turned, leaped — and, impossibly, brought the ball down in his mitt.

"Whoa! Would you look at that catch!" Coach yelled.

"Hey, hey, Doctor J.!" Larry Levine shouted.

"Doctor J.! I like it," Jordan said, clapping his hands.

"Hey, guys," Pete interrupted. "You know what? I think we've just found ourselves a new center fielder."

"Wait a minute," Jay Woo protested. "Does that mean I don't get to play center anymore?" Jay played center for two innings a game — or he had, until now.

"It means you'll all be playing a little less," Coach said. "If Jesus wants to play, I'll ask the league to let us add a new player midseason."

"Yeah!" the whole group of them roared.

"Fielders in for batting practice!" Coach yelled. "Hitters, take the field." Now everyone would get to see how Jesus — or Doctor J., as they'd all started calling him — handled the bat.

Jesus, hitting lefty, turned out to be a slap hitter. For his size, he didn't have a lot of power. But he seemed to be able to place the ball wherever he wanted to. He used the whole field, hitting it where the fielders weren't. He knew how to bunt, too, and with his speed, it was easy to see that he'd beat out a lot of infield grounders.

"He's an ideal leadoff hitter," Coach Bacino told Joey. "Thanks, kid. He's a real find. Think he'd like to be on the team?"

"Would he ever!" Joey said. "Yo, Jesus!"

Jesus was standing by home plate, surrounded by a circle of his brand-new friends. Suddenly he was the most popular kid around!

"Guess what?" Joey told him.

"I don't know. What?"

"You're on the team!"

Everyone cheered, and there were high fives all around. Jesus wasn't crying now. He was too busy enjoying the moment. So busy that he didn't even bother to thank Joey.

The Marlins' next game was on Saturday afternoon. Their opponents, the Yankees, were only 2–4, but the Marlins had not forgotten that the lowly Dodgers had almost beaten them. They were not about to let this game get away.

In a surprise decision, Coach Bacino decided to have Joey pitch the first three innings. "Just thought I'd shake things up a little" was the explanation — which explained nothing, as far as Joey could see. He'd gotten used to coming in to finish up the game. Now he'd have to get right out there, mentally unprepared, and do the job.

He was shaky from the start. Somehow, he couldn't seem to find the plate. He walked two out of the first three batters. When he finally did get the ball over, it was right down the middle of the plate, and the hitter sliced a hot line drive over the second baseman's head.

The ball had "inside-the-park home run" written all over it. But Jesus, like a bullet, got there in time to snag it on the fly, right at his shoe tops! In one fluid motion, he threw to second base, doubling up the runner who had gone to third, thinking there was no way that ball would be caught.

"Yes!" Joey screamed. "Incredible! A double play!" The spectators roared, and the Marlins jumped up and down in their excitement. "Jesus, you rule!"

The Yankees coach put his hands on his head. "Did you see that play?" he said to his assistant coach. "Who is that kid, anyway? Hey, Bacino!"

"Just moved to town," Coach Bacino yelled back from the Marlins bench. "Check with the league. We got an exemption, same as the Dodgers for their new pitcher."

The Yankee coach muttered something nasty and turned his attention back to the game. Joey walked the next hitter, and the next, and Coach Bacino came out to the mound.

"What's up with you today?" he asked Joey.

"I don't know."

"Just throw it over."

"But they'll clobber it," Joey protested. "They've got the bases loaded, Coach."

"Never mind. Just don't walk 'em home, okay? Make 'em earn it!"

"Okay." Joey concentrated on Pete's mitt and threw down the middle. The hitter swung and laced one right back at him. It bounced past him, past second base, and into center field, where Jesus grabbed it.

One runner had already scored. The kid behind him was around third base and on his way home when Jesus released his throw. It was a perfect bullet, on one hop, right into Pete's mitt. Pete tagged the runner in plenty of time. "Yer out!" the umpire called.

The inning was mercifully over. Joey knew he had Jesus to thank for getting out of it with only one run. Now it was time to get that run back.

Joey patted Jesus on the back. "You saved me!" he said.

"*De nada,*" Jesus said shyly. "I go bunt."

"Huh?"

"I bunt first pitch."

"Um, did Coach say to?"

"No to worry, I bunt. You see." He got up to the plate, and just as he'd promised, Jesus bunted the first pitch down the third-base line. It rolled to a stop right on the foul line. Jesus crossed first base before anyone even picked the ball up.

"Who *is* that kid?" the Yankee coach yelled again.

"His name is Jesus!" Coach Bacino called back, pronouncing it "GEE-zus."

"Very funny, Bacino. You're a regular laugh riot."

Jesus stole second base on the very next pitch. One out later, he stole third.

"How much you wanna bet he steals home?" Larry Levine said to the rest of them on the bench.

"No way," Pete said. "Nobody's ever done that in league play."

"Somebody must have done it, back in the day," Charlie said.

"I never heard of it being done," Larry said. "This kid is spooky good."

"And he's ours!" Jordan said, smiling. "Yeah, baby. We're number one."

Ellis Suggs struck out, and Matt Lowe came up to bat. The first pitch to him was in the dirt. Before the catcher had even started after the ball, Jesus was on his way home. "He's going! Cover! Cover!" yelled the Yankees coach.

The catcher grabbed the ball in his bare hand and lunged to tag Jesus. But the tag came too late — a nanosecond after Jesus's toe touched the plate. "Safe!" the umpire cried.

"Yeah! That's what I'm talkin' about!" Coach Bacino said, clapping. "Thank you, Jesus!"

"Hey, hey, Doctor J.!" Larry Levine chanted. "He's got the cure for what ails ya!"

Jesus was mobbed as he came back to the bench. Joey slapped him on the back, just like everyone else, but his mind was on his own failure. Even with Jesus's run, the game was still only tied. And Joey still hadn't figured out what was wrong with his pitching motion. By the time he'd pitched his full three innings, he'd walked in two more runs, and the Marlins were down, 3–1.

"Gallagher," Coach told him. "You sit out for a while, okay?"

"But Coach, I usually play center for three innings," Joey protested.

"Yeah, but I'm gonna ride the hot hand for now. Jesus is having himself a game, so I want to leave him out there."

Jesus made two more spectacular plays that day, had another infield single and a walk, and scored two more runs as the Marlins came back to win, 5–4. Coach Bacino gave him the game ball. Jesus was without a doubt the team's new star and everybody's hero.

As for Joey, who rode the bench the rest of the game, he was steaming inside. He was yesterday's hero, forgotten now. He'd nearly blown the game for them — for the second time in a row!

And who had taken his place in the spotlight? Jesus. Good old Doctor J. — with the nice new lefty glove Joey'd bought him. Tentacles of jealousy began to wrap themselves around his heart.

"Great game, Jesus," he muttered. Then he spat on the ground. Twice.

10

As soon as they got to school on Monday, Joey could sense the difference. Kids he knew only from playing baseball against them were coming up to them in the halls. Every single one of them wanted to talk to "Doctor J." Most of them ignored Joey in the crush to be "down" with Bordentown's newest baseball phenom.

"*Yo soy Antonio,*" Andy Norton said. "*Cómo estás tu?*"

"*Estoy bien,*" Jesus replied politely, accepting Andy's high five. "But my name no 'Doctor J.,' is Jesus."

"Sure, Doc," Charlie Morganstern said when Jesus told him the same thing. "Call me Carlos, yo. You and me, we're *amigos, sí?*"

"*Sí, sí,*" said Jesus, more than willing to accept all the attention he was getting — especially from the girls. They had obviously heard about Jesus's heroics on the ball field and wanted to check out the exotic new arrival on the scene. Never mind that he'd been there for almost a week and they hadn't looked at him twice, except to see if he was some kind of space alien.

Joey wished they would all just go away. But by lunch period, Jesus had been invited to three parties *and* a rock concert. He'd accepted every invitation — invitations that had not been extended to Joey. It was like Joey didn't even exist!

The worst part was, he had no one he could even talk to about it. Normally he would have sat down in a corner of the cafeteria with Larry Levine and complained to his heart's content. Larry would have made some funny jokes about it and done a great Jesus imitation. Joey would laugh, and soon he wouldn't feel so angry anymore.

But where was Larry now?

"Hey, hey, Doctor J.!" he was saying, slapping Jesus on the back as they met up on the lunch line. "Tacos today. Just like home, huh?"

"No," Jesus said with a sly smile that showed he knew Larry was kidding. "No like home. Here tacos no so good, I think."

"You think right, Doc," Larry congratulated him.

"I'd stay away from them if I were you. Try the chicken surprise. At least it'll be . . . well, surprising."

Yes, Jesus belonged to everybody now. He was everybody's new best friend. Even Larry's.

And Joey? He had exactly nobody. Not even Jesus.

When they got home after school, Joey's mom asked how everything was going. "Great," Joey mumbled and brushed past her, heading into the kitchen to get some snacks.

"Supercool," Jesus said. "I go three parties and also concert of Twisted Fyshburger!"

"Oh, my! Aren't you the social butterfly!" Joey's mom said admiringly. "I'm so glad you're having a good time, Jesus. The agency called today to see how you were doing, and I told them everything was fine, so I'm glad to see it really is."

"Yes. I very happy here," he said. "Joey very nice to me."

Joey, hearing this from the kitchen, slammed the peanut-butter jar down on the countertop. Good thing it was plastic, or it would have shattered all over the place.

"Everything all right in there, Joey?" his mom called.

"Fine," Joey said, gritting his teeth. "Everything's peachy," he muttered to himself.

Jesus came in. "We go practice soon, yes?" he asked.

Joey didn't answer. Instead, he concentrated on making himself a peanut butter and jelly sandwich.

"Everything is all right, yes?" Jesus asked, noticing Joey's silence.

"Yeah. Fine," Joey said, not looking up.

"No, I think is no fine," Jesus said.

"I said it's fine, and it's fine, okay?" Joey snapped back.

"I do something wrong?" Jesus asked.

"No. You're fine. You're great. You're perfect, okay? Have a good time at the parties and the concert."

"You come too?" Jesus asked, guessing at the reason for Joey's upset.

"Oh, yeah, sure," Joey replied. "Thanks but no thanks. I only go where I'm invited."

"I invite you," Jesus said.

"Yeah, thanks a bunch," Joey muttered. "But it's not the same thing."

"I no understand."

"Skip it, okay? Let's go to practice." Putting the jars back in the refrigerator, he slammed the door shut, grabbed his sandwich, and headed for the garage to get his mitt and bat.

At practice, Jesus was treated like a rock star. Half the kids on the team had figured out their Spanish names and were calling one another by them.

"Pedro!" Charlie called to home plate. "Heads up!"

"Okay, Carlos!" Pete yelled back. "Fire it in!"

When Jesus came up for his turn at batting practice, everyone started chanting, "Hey-SOOOOS! Hey-SOOOOS!" It sounded like they were booing, but of course they weren't. They were saluting their new hero.

Joey had had about all he could take. He knew the attention was fickle — that the first bad game Jesus had, it would all disappear like smoke. Still, it bothered him, like a thousand little needles pricking him under the skin. He knew he was close to blowing but didn't know how to prevent it.

It wasn't supposed to be like this. Jesus was supposed to be homesick and lonely. But now he had more friends than Joey!

Joey couldn't shake the thoughts that kept crowding his mind. He whiffed on most of his batting-practice swings, then took third base on the rotation as the right fielder came in to hit.

After the next batter, Joey moved to shortstop. Jesus was behind him in center field. Jordan cracked a shot right at Joey. Unprepared, his mind on Jesus, Joey muffed it, and the ball went by him. Jesus ran in to pick it up and throw it in. "You catch next time," he told Joey.

Jesus was trying to be nice, he knew. But Joey didn't feel like being nice back. When Jordan popped the next pitch up to short left center, Joey drifted back to catch it.

"Yo la tengo!" he heard Jesus call as he ran in for it.

But Joey kept drifting back as if he didn't hear him. As the ball came down, he stuck his mitt out. At the same time, he threw his weight backward, slamming into the onrushing Jesus. Unprepared for the impact, Jesus ricocheted backward, falling on his back and hitting his head on the ground.

Joey wasn't hurt at all by the accident. *And it* was *an accident,* he told himself. *Wasn't it?*

Apparently Jesus didn't think so. As he was helped to his feet, he stared at Joey. The hurt in his eyes was unmistakable.

103

"Sorry," Joey muttered. But Jesus didn't answer. Instead, he turned his back to Joey and slowly walked off the field.

"Hey, Doc, where ya goin'?" Larry Levine called after him from left field.

"Hey-SOOOOOS!" some of the others shouted. But Jesus wasn't listening. Dropping his mitt to the ground, he just kept walking until he reached the road, and then the corner. He disappeared around it.

"Hey, Gallagher, what's up with your boy?" Charlie asked.

"Why don't you go after him?" Pete suggested.

But Joey just stood there. "He's all right," Joey said, staring at the spot where Jesus had turned the corner. "Leave him alone. He'll work it out by himself."

"Maybe he's hurt," Jordan piped up.

"He's fine," Joey said through gritted teeth. "Now can we just play ball?"

"Why, Jesus, you haven't touched a bite of your dinner!" Joe's mom said as she looked at his plate. "Is something the matter?"

Jesus just shook his head.

"Aren't you hungry, son?" Joey's dad asked, concerned.

Jesus shook his head again but didn't say anything.

Joey's mom mouthed the word "homesick." Joey's dad nodded back, agreeing. But Joey knew better.

"I no hungry," Jesus said. "No feel so good. I go my room, okay?"

"Sure, Jesus, that's fine," said Joey's dad.

"Are you sick?" his mom asked.

"No sick . . . maybe . . . I no sure."

"Well, you go on upstairs," Joey's mom said. "I'll check on you in a while."

After Jesus left the dining room, they both started in on Joey. "What's going on with Jesus?" his dad demanded.

"How should I know?" Joey asked.

"Haven't you noticed anything at all?" his mom said, frowning.

"No!" Joey insisted. "Will you just get off it?"

"Is there something going on between you two?" his dad asked, scrutinizing Joey.

"No!" Joey held his ground. "I'm telling you, I don't know what's wrong with him. Maybe he's sick, like he says. Maybe he hates it here and wants to go home."

"Would you like it if he went home?" his dad asked.

The question pinned Joey to his seat. He didn't know how to answer it. Part of him did wish Jesus would just go away, that things would go back to the way they were before he came — with Joey as the new up-and-coming star of the Marlins. But another part of him — the part that had come to really like Jesus — didn't feel that way at all.

That part of him felt rotten for bumping into Jesus on purpose. Rotten for wishing him gone. Rotten for being rotten. "I'm not feeling so well either," he said, throwing his napkin down and getting up to go. "I'm going to bed, okay?"

"Okay, Joey," his mom said. "Do you want some pain reliever?"

"No, I'll be okay," he said. "I just . . . overdid it at practice, that's all." As he left the room, he could feel his parents' eyes burning a hole in the back of his head.

It was wrong of him, he knew. But how could he help the way he felt?

11

By Tuesday afternoon, Joey had managed to calm himself down somewhat. He knew that no matter how irritated he got at Jesus, he mustn't say or do anything stupid, anything that made him look like a jerk.

He'd gotten through the whole day at school pretty well, ignoring all the attention his "brother" was getting. Brianne had flirted with Jesus like crazy at lunch, practically begging him to ask her to the movies, but Jesus had no clue what was going on. How could he have known? The signals were obvious to any American kid, but Joey realized it must be totally different in Nicaragua.

The only one — other than Joey — who still seemed to have something against Jesus was Damon Krupp. Joey had stuck up for Jesus that day in the cafeteria. Would he do the same now? He wasn't so sure.

Joey and Jesus rode their bikes to the field after school. Several times along the way, Joey took off at full speed, getting far ahead. Jesus didn't even try to catch up. Joey knew he was acting like a baby, but he just couldn't stop himself.

The regular baseball season was winding down, with only three games to go. With a record of 6–1, the Marlins were tied for first with the Orioles and the Twins, a team they were scheduled to play next week. If the Marlins won two of their last three games, they'd be in the play-offs. They'd also have Nicky Canelo back, and that meant it would be clear sailing all the way to the championship.

Coach Bacino approached them as soon as they arrived at the field for their game with the 4–3 Brewers. "Listen," he told Joey. "Matt Lowe's not gonna be here."

"What?" Joey said. "Why? What's wrong with him?"

"Emergency appendectomy," the coach said grimly. "He's out for the season."

"No!" Joey cried. "What are we gonna do?"

"I know," the coach said. "It's just bad luck — a rash of injuries. It can happen to any team, and we're just gonna have to fight through it." He kicked at the dirt, obviously worried. "So here's how we're gonna play it.

Gallagher, you'll pitch the first three. Jesus — you said you pitched in your country?"

"*Sí!*" Jesus said. "I pitch for team! Very good!"

"Okay, then, you're it," Coach said, slapping Jesus on the back. "Let's see what you can do."

Joey could practically feel the steam coming out of his ears. How come Jesus got to pitch the last three innings without even trying out?

He got up on the mound angry and promptly got into trouble because he was throwing too hard. As a result, his pitches were flat — very hittable. Before the first half inning was over, the Marlins were down, 2–0.

Luckily, Jesus got a rally started right away, with a perfect bunt and a steal to second base. After Joey struck out swinging, Jordan Halpin knocked Jesus in with a single. Charlie Morganstern hit a home run over the center fielder's head, and the Marlins were back in the lead.

But they held the lead only for the moment. In the top of the second, Joey walked two batters and allowed a double to left that scored two runs. It was 4–3, Brewers, and that was the way it stayed through the end of the third inning.

That inning, Joey had given up three singles without

yielding a run — but only because Jesus (who else?) had nailed a runner at the plate with a perfect strike from shallow center field. When Joey struck out the cleanup hitter for the third out of the inning, the whole Marlins team let out a roar, and everyone congratulated him for a job well done.

In the bottom of the third, Jesus started another rally, with a slap double down the third-base line. This time, Joey made contact on his turn at bat, blooping a single behind third base. Jesus, with his blinding speed, scored all the way from second. Joey, the RBI man, took second on the throw to the plate and scored when Jordan singled behind him. Once again, the Marlins were in the lead, 5–4.

Now it was Jesus's job to hold the lead. Joey had never seen him pitch before. During their practices in the driveway, Jesus had never even gone into a windup. But he had one, all right. An unforgettable one.

Jesus stared in at the plate, cap pulled down over his eyes, hands together and low. As he went into his windup, he turned toward first base and lifted his hands high over his head as his knee came all the way up to his face. Then, in a blur, his whole body whipped around, and his long left arm swung sidearm. The ball came in surprisingly fast, rising as it went, popping loudly into Pete's catcher's mitt.

As impressive as it was to Joey and the rest of the Marlins, Jesus's pitching was a total shock to the poor Brewers. They went down swinging, one after the other. The inning ended after only eleven pitches, nine of them strikes. "Awesome!" Coach Bacino yelled. "Absolutely incredible!"

The legend of Jesus was growing by the minute, and Joey could feel his own jealousy rising to fever pitch. The next inning was not quite as spectacular — Jesus threw fourteen pitches — but he still struck out all three Brewers he faced. Six in a row, with three to go. Could he possibly do it a third time?

When the Marlins went down in the fifth without scoring a run, they were still clinging to their one-run lead. Now the Brewers came up for their last licks. For two innings, they'd whiffed at Jesus's pitches, fooled by all the motion in his windup and frozen by the rising action of his fastball.

Now, as they tried to adjust, Jesus started mixing in a change-up, varying the speed of his pitches. It was too much for the Brewers. They went down one-two-three — nine batters faced, nine spectacular strikeouts for Jesus. It was as good as anything Nicky Canelo had ever done.

All the Marlins mobbed Jesus, screaming their heads off for their new superstar. Even Nicky Canelo, still a spectator, whooped it up with the rest of them.

Only Joey did not join in the general celebration. He threw down his mitt, then picked it up and headed for the bike rack, unnoticed and ignored by his ecstatic teammates. Only one set of eyes was fixed on him. Sad, rejected eyes boring right through the back of his head.

Jesus's eyes.

12

Joey did not go directly home. Instead, he pedaled over to Marx's Luncheonette. Parking his bike, he went inside, sat on one of the stools at the counter, and ordered himself a double-chocolate malted.

How had it come to this? He'd never really been all that interested in having an exchange student come to live with them. Joey had nothing against Jesus personally. It was just the way he'd stolen Joey's thunder. Stepped into his spotlight and gotten all the attention that should have been Joey's.

Well, it wasn't working out, that was for sure. That was what it all came down to. Joey tried to imagine going to his mom and dad and telling them to send Jesus back to Nicaragua. "It would be better for everybody," he would say.

Yeah, right. That would work — *not.* He tried to sip

on his malted through a straw, but the straw quickly became clogged with thick chocolate ice cream. Ah, Marx's malteds — one of life's little treats. Joey grabbed a spoon and started to eat the malted instead of drinking it.

The front door of the luncheonette opened, and the little sleigh bells Mr. Marx had attached to the door tinkled brightly. In walked Larry Levine. He took the seat next to Joey.

"Some game, huh?" he said, trying a smile out on Joey.

Joey didn't smile back. "Yeah. Great," he said.

"One more win and we're in the play-offs!" Larry said.

"Whoopee," Joey said, stuffing his gullet with a gob of ice cream.

"You sound underwhelmed."

"Inside, I'm jumping up and down for joy," Joey told him, still staring at his malted.

"Man, that Jesus is something!" Larry said. Joey's wince did not escape him. "You mad at him or something?"

"Me? Nah."

"Oh. Okay."

"Why would I be mad?"

"Beats me. I thought maybe you'd be able to supply the reason."

Joey turned to him. "Is that supposed to be funny?"

"Not exactly." Larry ordered a soda, then turned back to face Joey. "Look, it's none of my business. I'm only your close friend. But even I can see that something's going on between you two."

"You can, huh?"

"No doubt about it. So, did he do something bad? You can tell me. I can keep a secret."

"Not really," Joey said. "I just don't like how he showboats, you know?"

"Showboats? I don't follow you."

"Like when he does something good on the field or at the plate. You know."

"What, he cheers? Does a little dance? Hey, who doesn't these days? If I ever did anything good on a baseball field, I'd stand on my head and cluck like a chicken."

"Remind me to bring the video camera," Joey said, smiling in spite of himself.

"So, you don't like him showboating, huh? I don't know. Don't you think you're being a little . . . over-sensitive?"

"Right. It's all me, okay? My bad. So shoot me." Joey pushed his half-finished malted away and got up to go.

"I didn't say that," Larry said. "All I mean is, maybe you should cut the kid a little slack, you know? He's here, what, two weeks? He's down with the kids here. I'll bet that's a pretty good feeling when you're from far away and don't know anybody."

"You're right, okay? I'll see you," Joey said, heading for the door.

"You know, I hope you don't hate me for saying this, but you looked happier when everyone was making fun of his name."

Joey froze at the door, stung by the truth of Larry's words. He *had* liked it better then — back when he was Jesus's only friend and chief protector. He remembered Jesus's sense of wonder when he'd first seen Joey's house; when he'd been presented with Sandy's old bike; when Joey had given him his first real baseball mitt. It had been for the wrong hand, sure, but Jesus had been so touched by the gift that he cried.

Jesus didn't *need* Joey anymore. That was it. *That*

was why Joey was mad at him. Larry had hit the nail right on the head. Slowly Joey turned and walked back over to the counter. "You know, where he grew up, they used cereal boxes for mitts?" he told Larry as he sat back down.

"No lie?"

"Word. He cut up one of our boxes with kitchen shears, making holes for the fingers, you know?"

"Wow."

"He'd never even heard of a mall," Joey went on. Larry shook his head in wonder. "And when we gave him Sandy's old bomb of a bike to ride, he couldn't believe it."

"Really, we forget how lucky we are here in America," Larry said, staring at his soda and nodding slowly.

"Totally," Joey agreed. "His whole family lives in a two-room house, and there are like, nine of them or something. He was telling me that lots of houses there have dirt floors. He said he thought his family was pretty rich because they had a tile floor and a bathroom out back. When he first got off the plane, he was, like, whistling at all the big houses."

"I guess they are pretty big, by world standards," Larry agreed. "It's easy to forget that."

"Yeah."

Suddenly it seemed to Joey that having Jesus as a houseguest was a gift, not a burden. "Hey, Lar?"

"Yeah?"

"Thanks."

"For what?"

"For reminding me." He went out the door, ignoring the puzzled look on Larry's face.

"Reminding you about what?" Larry called after him.

"That it's not all about me. It's about Jesus, too."

He walked over to his bike, tethered to a parking meter by the street.

Yeah, Jesus, he reminded himself. *Jesus, who was so grateful to get the gift you gave him that he didn't say anything about it being for the wrong hand. Jesus, who sooo didn't want to hurt your feelings that he tried to learn to play ball right-handed. Jesus, who wanted so much for you to like him that he carved that tiny little family for you, with you and him in it, side by side. Jesus, who was willing to change his name because it bothered you — not him, but you — that a bunch of nitwits were teasing him about it. That Jesus. The kid who came all the way to a foreign country and*

118

trusted you to look after him. Well, you're not doing too good a job, are you?

Getting back on the bike, Joey hit the kickstand and headed home. He had some urgent repair work to do. Things were going to be different from here on in.

He left his bike in the driveway and went inside, but no one seemed to be home. He knew both his parents were working that day and wouldn't be home till just before dinnertime. So he wasn't expecting them to be around. But where was Jesus?

"Jesus?" he called. No answer. He went up to Jesus's room and knocked on the door. Nothing.

Joey opened the door and peeked inside. There, on the neatly made bed, was an open suitcase filled with all Jesus's clothes!

"Jesus? You here?" He entered the room and looked around some more. The dresser drawers were all open and mostly empty. The photos of home Jesus had brought with him were gone — presumably wrapped in something and stuffed in the suitcase.

In the wastebasket at the foot of the desk was the cardboard mitt Jesus had made out of a cereal box. Joey picked it out, wanting to save it from oblivion. It was a pretty neat trick, after all, making a mitt out of a cardboard box. Then he saw that there was something else in the wastebasket — the brand-new mitt he'd bought Jesus!

Joey felt like he'd been punched in the stomach. He hadn't meant to hurt Jesus's feelings like this.

Sure you did, he told himself. *You jerk.*

Only he hadn't realized quite how badly Jesus would be wounded by his rejection.

On the desk was a folded note with FOR JOEY written on the outside. Joey picked it up and read it:

I think you no like Jesus. Maybe is my name. Maybe I should have change like you wanted. I sorry for I come here. In my country is beautiful and everyone nice. In America, is very rich and beautiful, and many people friendly, but some people not so much. Some people no like boy from other country. I want go home to my family now. Before, I want this be my second home, my second family, but now I think is mistake. Good-bye, Joey.

Jesus

Joey stared at the note in his hands, and then a drop of water hit it. A tear. Joey hadn't even realized he was crying. He wiped his eyes, but they kept watering anyway. "Jerk. You idiot," he told himself.

And then he noticed the open window. Joey poked his head outside. The window opened out onto the gently sloping roof of the back porch. There, sitting with his knees up near his chin and his arms clasped around them, was Jesus.

"Hey!" Joey said.

Jesus turned to look at him with his big, sad brown eyes. Then he looked away again, staring out into the distance.

Joey climbed out onto the roof and squatted next to Jesus. "I said hey," he repeated. "Wuzzup?"

Jesus didn't respond, so Joey went on. "Look, I'm sorry, okay? I've been acting really mean, and I've got no reason for it. I'm just a jerk, all right? But I'm not gonna be like that anymore."

Jesus said nothing.

"I'm just spoiled and selfish," Joey continued. "I guess a lot of us here can be that way sometimes. We've got so much, and everybody we know has so much, that we forget that it's not like that everywhere. I . . . I thought, when you came here, that I was going to show you everything . . . teach you stuff about America . . . but it winds up you're the one who's teaching me."

Jesus still didn't say a word. The silence stretched for a long moment, then Joey said quietly, "Don't leave, okay? I . . . I want you to stay here the whole year."

Jesus finally looked at him. He searched Joey's face, then slowly nodded. "All right," he said. "I stay."

"Great! And Jesus, I'm sorry about —"

"Is okay."

"You sure?"

"I sure." There was a long silence. "But only one thing . . ."

"What?"

"I no like this name, 'Doctor J.' I no doctor. My name Jesus. Why they call me this 'Doctor J.?'"

"They're gonna call you whatever they want, man," Joey told him with a shrug. "But I promise you, *I'm* always gonna call you by your name. Jesus. Because you're fine with me just the way you are."

Jesus smiled, reached out, and put a hand on Joey's

shoulder. "After one year, when I go back, you come visit my country and stay with my family. My country very beautiful. Much good *béisbol* also."

Joey smiled and wiped the dried tears off his face with his sleeve. "Yeah?"

"Yes. But I think in Nicaragua, we call you José, *sí?*" Jesus reached out and ruffled Joey's hair, and the two boys burst out laughing.

"Come on," Joey said. "Let's go inside and get you unpacked."

13

Saturday afternoon was the big game with the Twins. With both teams' records at 7–1 (same as the Orioles, whose lone loss had been to the Marlins), the winner of today's game was guaranteed a spot in the best-of-three championship series.

When they saw Joey and Jesus approaching, the whole team ran over to greet them. "Hey, hey, Doctor J.!" Larry Levine said, high-fiving Jesus. "Marlins are gonna win today!"

"Yo, Doc!" Charlie Morganstern said, clapping Jesus on the back. "How's the arm?"

"Is good," Jesus said, smiling. "I feel good today."

"Me too," said Joey, though no one had asked him. He didn't mind anymore if Jesus got all the attention. Didn't mind a bit.

Nicky Canelo was there, too. "You guys make the

championship series, and I'll be ready for it," he promised. "Just get us there, okay?"

"It's not gonna be easy," Pete Alessandra said. "Jordan's sick, Jay Woo's visiting his cousins in San Francisco, and Matt Lowe's gone, of course . . ."

It was going to be a wounded, limping Marlins team that went to battle today. Coach Bacino gathered them all together. "I'm gonna need maximum effort from everybody," he said. "Gallagher, you start on the mound. Jesus, I know you're a lefty — but can you play shortstop?"

"*Sí*, I play good," Jesus said, and everyone laughed.

"I'll bet you do," Pete said.

"Modest, too," Charlie joked.

"We'll reverse it after three innings," Coach went on.

"What about center field?" Joey asked.

The coach shrugged. "I guess it's you, Levine."

"Me?" Larry pointed to his own chest. "Are you sure?"

"Hey," the coach said sternly. "No joking around. There's nobody else. I need you to give me a good game out there today. Can you do it?"

"Uh, sure," Larry said, sounding less than convinced.

The game began, with Joey on the mound and Jesus anchoring the infield at short. Knowing that his outfield was suspect, Joey tried to keep his pitches low so he'd get a lot of ground balls. This worked well for the first two hitters. Then Damon Krupp came up to the plate.

Joey flashed back to that first day in the school cafeteria, when Damon had taunted Jesus and later doused Joey's shirt with chocolate pudding. It made Joey mad just thinking of it. And thinking of it must have caused his arm to shift just slightly, because on the first pitch, Joey uncorked a fastball that hit Damon squarely on the behind.

"Hey!" he shouted angrily. "He did that on purpose!" He threw down his helmet and bat and started walking toward the mound.

Joey panicked, frozen in place. Damon was much, much bigger than he was, but if he ran, everyone would laugh at him. So he just stood there, too scared to even raise his fists in self-defense.

"Yo!" the umpire shouted, racing out in time to catch Damon just before he reached Joey. "Yo, chill, okay? Just take your base now."

Damon, still staring at Joey, walked slowly to first, limping slightly and rubbing his behind. Joey blew out

126

a relieved breath and turned to face the next Twins hitter. Only now his heart was beating so hard and so fast that he couldn't put the ball over the plate. He wound up walking the next two batters, loading the bases.

Coach Bacino ran out to the mound. "Hey, take it easy, okay?" he told Joey. "Just calm down and throw strikes."

"I can't!" Joey said. "I'm trying, okay? It just isn't happening."

"Look, forget about the kid you hit, Gallagher. That's over. You've got two outs. Concentrate and let them hit the ball. You've got fielders behind you."

Joey wound up slowly and aimed for the center of the plate. He threw a slow change-up, but the batter wasn't fooled. He hit a long fly ball to center field. Larry Levine looked up, shaded his eyes with his mitt, and then threw up his hands, indicating he'd lost the ball in the sun.

Ellis Suggs tried to run over and make the play, but he was too late. By the time he picked up the ball and threw it back in, two runs had scored, and the hitter was on second with a double that should have been the third out.

Joey got the next hitter to ground to short. Jesus

made the throw to first base to end the inning, but now it was 2–0, Twins. Joey and the Marlins had dug themselves a big hole to climb out of.

Now they got to see why the Twins were a winning team. Their pitcher was nearly six feet tall and threw so fast that the ball was a blur. The Marlins went down swinging one after the other — even Jesus.

For three innings, they went hitless, managing just one walk. On the other side, Joey held the Twins scoreless — except for Damon Krupp, who hit a monster home run off Joey his second time up. He practically walked around the bases, pointing at Joey and talking trash.

"Hey, you no talk like that," Jesus said as Damon passed him on his way around the bases. "Is no nice."

"Shut up, you Spanish fly," Damon shot back, giving Jesus a little push. The umpire had his back turned and didn't see it, but Coach Bacino did. He raced down the bench, yelling in vain for Damon to be tossed from the game.

Jesus took over the pitching duties in the fourth inning, but he, too, seemed rattled by Damon's actions. He gave up three hits and a run before settling down to retire the side.

It was now the bottom of the fourth inning, and the new Twins pitcher took the mound. He didn't throw as fast as their first pitcher, but his ball had a deceptive movement to it that made it hard to hit. The Marlins got two men on base, but they failed to score when Huey Brewster's long fly ball was run down and caught by the left fielder.

The fifth inning began with the Marlins down, 4–0. The first batter up in the inning was Damon Krupp, and he started right in again with the trash talking. "Hey, Jesus!" he yelled to the mound, pronouncing it "GEE-zus." "If I pray hard enough, will you throw me a meatball?"

"Shut up, punk!" Joey yelled back from his short-stop position.

"No, you shut up," Damon shot back. "You nailed me once already. You looking for a little payback?"

"Play ball!" the umpire ordered.

Jesus threw a fastball inside, and Damon jumped back to get out of the way. "That's it," he said as he charged the mound. "I'm gonna make a Spanish ome-let out of you."

"Hey!" Joey yelled, throwing down his mitt and run-ning to protect Jesus. He barreled into Damon just before Damon reached Jesus. Both boys went down in a heap, with Joey and Damon pummeling each other furiously and everyone else trying to pry them apart.

"Break it up! Break it up!" the umpire shouted. "You're both out! Ejected!"

"You leave him alone," Joey growled, feeling the pain everywhere.

"What do you care, you dweeb?" Damon asked, wiping the blood from his nose. "What is he, your brother or something?"

Joey nodded. "Yeah. That's right. He's my brother, okay?"

Damon shook his head, dusted himself off, and headed for the bench. Joey did the same.

Jesus ran after him. "Joey!"

Joey stopped to look back at him. "Yeah?"

"You okay?"

Joey smiled. "Never been better."

Coach Bacino wasn't smiling, though. "Great. You got yourself kicked out of a crucial game. I hope you're proud of yourself."

Joey didn't answer, but the truth was, he *was* proud of himself. He'd stood up for his "brother," and if he'd had it to do all over again, he would have done exactly the same thing. "Come on, Jesus!" he yelled. "Win this one for us!"

Jesus looked at him and nodded. "No worry, *amigo*. I win it for *you*." With that, he proceeded to strike out the side one-two-three, fooling the Twins hitters with his dazzling windup and deceptive delivery.

In the bottom of the fifth, Jesus was in the middle of a Marlins rally. Larry Levine, of all people, got it started with a one-out single that he dribbled into no-man's-land between the pitcher and the first baseman. Ellis Suggs walked. Jesus came up with one out and two men on, and launched a line shot into left field. Two runs scored, and Jesus came around later on a two-out single by Charlie Morganstern. The team managed two more walks, but they were stranded when Huey struck out.

They were only one run behind now, and Jesus made sure it stayed that way through the sixth by striking out the side for the second inning in a row.

Now it was time for the Marlins' last licks — their last shot at securing a play-off berth out of this game.

Damon Krupp was hollering abuse at Jesus from the Twins bench for all he was worth.

"Hey, Coach!" Coach Bacino yelled to the Twins

coach. "How about showing a little class, huh?" The Twins coach made a hostile gesture in return. "All right, that does it," Bacino muttered. "These guys are going down. Come on, Pete, get us started."

Pete obliged, smacking a hard single through the middle. Larry then struck out, but Pete managed to steal second on the last pitch. "That's the way!" Coach Bacino yelled, clapping his hands. "Come on, team!"

Ellis Suggs got up to bat — last in the order and probably least likely of all the Marlins to get a hit. Except he did. He blooped one right over the third baseman's head, and it bounced fair before kicking into foul territory.

Everyone was screaming at the top of his lungs as Pete took off for third. The throw got there a second before Pete, but the shortstop bobbled it, and Pete was safe.

Ellis, however, was still stuck halfway between first and second, and the alert Twins shortstop threw to second. The second baseman ran right at poor Ellis, who stood there, frozen in embarrassment and confusion, and was tagged for the second out of the inning.

Coach Bacino and the entire Marlins team let out a moan of agony. So close, and yet so far!

There was Pete, only a base away from tying the game, but they only had one out left. Jesus came to the plate, and Joey could see the fierce look of determination in his eyes. "Go, Jesus!" he yelled at the top of his lungs.

If Jesus heard, he gave no sign. Instead, he bunted the first pitch — a perfect bunt right up the first-base line. The catcher started after it, but when Pete broke from third base for home, the pitcher yelled for the catcher to cover.

The pitcher picked up the ball and flipped it to the catcher, but the tag on Pete was a fraction of a second too late. "Safe!" yelled the umpire, and the game was tied, 4–4. Not only that, but in the confusion, Jesus made it all the way to second!

"Attababy!" Coach Bacino yelled, clapping his hands.

"Hey, hey, Doctor J.!" Larry shouted. "Whoo-oo!"

"My man!" Charlie called, clapping and whistling.

Joey whooped and hollered. "Go, Jesus!" He looked across at Damon, who was kicking something in his frustration and fury.

Jesus took a long lead, and on the second pitch, he took off for third base. The catcher fired a strike to third, but Jesus was so fast and had gotten such a good jump that he made it safely under the tag.

Now all they needed was a hit. The batter wiggled the bat over his head and waited for the next pitch.

Only it never came. As the pitcher was about to go into his windup, Jesus broke for home. The pitcher reacted, faking a throw to third. When Jesus broke back, the pitcher fired to third base, and Jesus took off toward home again. The third baseman caught the ball and fired toward the catcher. Wild throw! As the catcher scrambled to find the ball, Jesus kept going. The catcher dug the ball out of the dirt, but it was way too late. Jesus crossed the plate safely, and the game was over!

"Did you see that?" Coach Bacino yelled to no one in particular. "He stole home!"

Jesus disappeared in a pile of happy Marlins, and Joey was in there too, yelling to beat the band along with the rest of them.

The Marlins were in the championship series, and Nicky Canelo would soon be back, making them nearly unbeatable. Even better, Jesus had won the game for them — and for *him*.

"You did it!" he told a happy Jesus as he pulled him from the bottom of the pile. "You really did it!"

"I say I win game for you," Jesus said bashfully. "You see I no lie."

"Way to go — brother," Joey said.

"Thank you — brother," Jesus replied. Joey knew that Jesus wasn't his real brother, but that didn't matter anymore. He felt like one, and that was the important thing. As the two boys hugged each other tightly, Joey knew that no one and nothing would succeed in turning them against each other ever again.

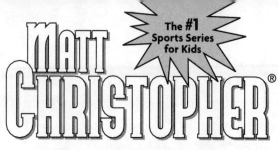

The #1 Sports Series for Kids

Read them all!

*Originally published as *Crackerjack Halfback*

All available in paperback from Little, Brown and Company

Matt Christopher®

Lance Armstrong

Kobe Bryant

Jennifer Capriati

Terrell Davis

Julie Foudy

Jeff Gordon

Wayne Gretzky

Ken Griffey Jr.

Mia Hamm

Tony Hawk

Grant Hill

Ichiro

Derek Jeter

Randy Johnson

Michael Jordan

Mario Lemieux

Tara Lipinski

Mark McGwire

Greg Maddux

Hakeem Olajuwon

Shaquille O'Neal

Alex Rodriguez

Curt Schilling

Briana Scurry

Sammy Sosa

Venus and
Serena Williams

Tiger Woods

Steve Young